Nico frowned. "You look terrified."

Grace gulped and jumped again at another crack of thunder and then at the sound of rain racing along the walls and on the roof, as ferocious as the sound of a thundering waterfall. She felt as though the entire structure of the building was going to cave in.

And the temperature seemed to have dropped. Or was that her imagination? She couldn't move a muscle.

"I'm fine," she breathed, her voice staccato with fear.

She stepped toward Nico. She was barely aware of doing so.

She cried out when thunder ripped through the room again and lightning flashed as bright as a sudden blaze of fire.

And just like that, several things happened at once. She moved at the same time as her boss, fear meeting strength, panic rushing into the arms of calm as he enfolded her.

Everything faded. The howling of the wind...the clatter of rain...the terrifying darkness of day that had suddenly turned to night.

Grace held on to him. Her arms snaked around his whipcord-lean body and she felt the hardness of muscle pressed against her, strong and comforting.

Cathy Williams can remember reading Harlequin books as a teenager, and now that she is writing them, she remains an avid fan. For her, there is nothing like creating romantic stories and engaging plots, and each and every book is a new adventure. Cathy lives in London, and her three daughters—Charlotte, Olivia and Emma—have always been, and continue to be, the greatest inspirations in her life.

Books by Cathy Williams

Harlequin Presents

The Forbidden Cabrera Brother
Desert King's Surprise Love-Child
Consequences of Their Wedding Charade
Hired by the Forbidden Italian
Bound by a Nine-Month Confession

Secrets of the Stowe Family

Forbidden Hawaiian Nights
Promoted to the Italian's Fiancée
Claiming His Cinderella Secretary

Visit the Author Profile page
at Harlequin.com for more titles.

Cathy Williams

A WEEK WITH THE FORBIDDEN GREEK

HARLEQUIN®
PRESENTS™

Recycling programs
for this product may
not exist in your area.

ISBN-13: 978-1-335-73879-0

A Week with the Forbidden Greek

Copyright © 2022 by Cathy Williams

All rights reserved. No part of this book may be used or reproduced in
any manner whatsoever without written permission except in the case of
brief quotations embodied in critical articles and reviews.

This is a work of fiction. Names, characters, places and incidents
are either the product of the author's imagination or are used fictitiously.
Any resemblance to actual persons, living or dead, businesses,
companies, events or locales is entirely coincidental.

For questions and comments about the quality of this book,
please contact us at CustomerService@Harlequin.com.

Harlequin Enterprises ULC
22 Adelaide St. West, 41st Floor
Toronto, Ontario M5H 4E3, Canada
www.Harlequin.com

Printed in U.S.A.

A WEEK WITH THE FORBIDDEN GREEK

CHAPTER ONE

NICO SPOTTED HER long before she spotted him, but because he wasn't expecting his prim and proper secretary to be *in a bar*, it took him a few seconds for his brain to compute what his eyes were seeing.

Grace? His efficient, predictable and, oh, so self-contained personal assistant? Here? In this smoky, dark, sultry jazz bar in Mayfair? Surely not!

Framed in one of the three old-fashioned arched doorways that opened into a room that was very cleverly arranged around a highly polished bar and a bandstand, Nico straightened and narrowed his eyes.

Next to him, his date for the evening was clutching his arm and gazing up at him.

Nico should have been in New York for three days but the main guy on the other side of the Atlantic had cancelled because his wife had been rushed to hospital and it had seemed pointless to make the trip in his absence.

So here he was. A last-minute arrangement with a woman who had been texting him with intent ever since they had been introduced two months ago at a fundraiser in Mayfair.

Now, Nico utterly forgot the blonde at his side. Every ounce of his attention homed in on his secretary with an intensity that made his breathing slow and set up a steady drumbeat in his temples.

The soulful, sexy tempo of the background jazz faded.

The waiters swerving between tables and round sofas with their large, circular trays of food and drink disappeared.

The soft, feminine, flirty purring of the woman next to him was suddenly an irritating background noise.

Grace Brown, *his* Grace Brown, wore knee-length skirts in riveting shades of grey and beige.

She always, *but always*, kept her hair tied back. Severely.

Her shoes were always sensible. Practical, *sensible* pumps with just the smallest of heels.

And above all else, no make-up.

Sure, she'd attended the occasional conference with him but the uniform had never changed.

Even on her thirtieth birthday a little over a year ago, which he had personally arranged as a surprise do at one of the high-end restaurants not a million miles away from his towering glass office building, she had *still* been in her stalwart knee-length skirt and beige jumper and cardigan.

So who the heck was this woman sitting at the table at the back, reaching for the glass of wine in front of her?

Not even the subdued, atmospheric lighting in the room could disguise the fact that she was *in a dress*. Something with thin straps that showed off slim shoulders, and her hair was loose, a thick fall of chestnut that highlighted her cheekbones and softened the austere look he had become so accustomed to. The table obscured all but her top half and yet Nico's curious, stunned dark gaze still dropped, searching to unearth the slender body encased in the floral, frothy summer dress.

He was so enthralled by the sight of her, so transported by what even he realised was an unreasonable degree of sheer shock at seeing her out of context, that it took him a while to register that there was something a little off with what he was seeing.

She was with some guy.

The man floated into his vision as an afterthought even though he was sitting adjacent to her.

Receding hairline...one hand on a glass of something that looked like whisky and the other reaching towards her even as she skittered back and tucked her hair nervously behind one ear.

People coming and going interrupted his view, but he felt something slither down his spine because he knew her almost better than he knew himself.

The hair might be tantalisingly loose, and she might be in a dress that did all sorts of things to his imagination, but she was still *his* Grace Brown and he could pick up that infinitesimal tremor in the hand holding the wine glass, the nervous licking of her lips as she pulled back.

Discomfort poured off her in waves and Nico was suddenly galvanised into the sort of caveman protective mode that he would never have credited himself as having in a million years.

'I have to go.' He turned to his date and raked his fingers through his dark hair, barely able to focus on the blonde standing next to him, itching to glance back to the unfolding scene at the table at the back.

'What?'

'You have my apologies.' It wasn't her fault, and he was gentleman enough to admit that, just as he was honest enough to also acknowledge that he was doing her a favour.

They weren't going to end up in bed, however luscious the curves. The evening would conclude in disappointment for her and relief for him as they went their separate ways.

'Why do you have to go? We've just got here!'

'I know. I'll get my driver to take you back to your place.'

'But look at me! I'm all dressed for a night out!'

'And you look spectacular.'

'I don't mind waiting for you! I'll… I'll…just sit at the bar until you've done whatever you have to do!'

'It's better for you to return to your apartment.'

'Will you at least meet me there later?'

'If I were to be polite, I would say *perhaps*. If I were to be honest, I would have to say *no*. I'm an honest man.'

'But…'

'I have to go, Clarissa.' This as he was urgently

texting his driver, who was on standby, to head right back to the bar so that he could collect her. He tucked his mobile into his pocket. 'Sid will be here in ten. He'll wait for you outside.'

'Thanks for nothing, Nico!'

No point going for another apology. Truth was… Clarissa wasn't going to lose sleep over a broken date, even one she had been angling for for a while. She would flounce off and, within an hour, would be on the phone to one of her model friends probably slagging him off.

Besides, gut instinct about Grace and whoever she was with was already consuming his attention and he barely glanced at Clarissa's departing back before striding off into the dark room and amongst the crowds and straight to that table at the back.

Grace had no idea that her boss was in the crowd, far less that he had spotted her from the across the room.

She was too busy trying to work out how best to extricate herself from her evening.

How on earth could this have gone so wrong?

The profile had looked *so* promising!

Victor Blake: aged thirty-four.
Occupation: lawyer.
Hobbies: theatre, foreign movies and reading.

Six foot three with a full head of hair and a smile that crinkled his eyes, at least in the photo that he had posted of himself standing in front of a sailboat, which had implied a love of the ocean, presumably.

Grace couldn't have been more cautious. Three weeks of emails and several conversations before dinner had been suggested by him at this very venue. Grace had been impressed. She'd never been here but she'd booked it often enough for her boss. Chez Giscard…an uber-expensive jazz club in the heart of Mayfair. She had been thrilled.

First date in for ever with someone she had so much in common with. How awful could it be?

She loved the theatre even though she couldn't actually remember the last time she'd been. She enjoyed foreign films. She read voraciously, largely when she was guiltily aware that she should be going out…and sailing? Well, the very thought of it was enticing. Who would ever object to the wind blowing through their hair and the salty air against their face?

So how was it that she was now sitting here, toying with the stem of her wine glass, her anxiety levels rising in small, incremental degrees as her date poured drink after drink for himself and tried to edge closer and closer?

This was Grace's first foray into the thorny business of trying to find a guy via a checklist of likes and dislikes, dispassionately listed under various Soulmate Perfect headings. It was a world she had never seriously considered exploring until six months ago when she had looked in the mirror and staring back at her had been a woman now in her thirties with next to no experience of the opposite sex. A woman who had spent her life juggling various responsibilities that had landed on her shoulders, almost without her realising their consequences at the time.

A woman who could proudly look back on her youth as a time spent anxiously looking out for her mum and then, later, her brother.

Whatever the opposite of a misspent youth was, she had lived it.

And to top it all off, all those years... *four and a half of them*...spent with a crazy crush on her boss.

She'd been hiding. Life had been happening out there but she had turned her back on it and, instead, taken the easier option of a forbidden attraction that was safe because it would never come to anything.

Except, time was gathering pace. She had found her first grey hair and had realised with shock that if she wasn't careful, she would find herself staring in that very same mirror in ten years' time and the only difference might be that the single grey hair had multiplied and taken over.

So here she was, getting her life back on track.

She felt the clammy hand of her date slap down on her thigh and she squirmed away with palpable distaste.

They'd exhausted polite conversation and for the life of her she couldn't think of anything to say. When he leaned in and asked her where they could go from here, she stared at him with alarm because she knew exactly what direction the conversation was now beginning to head.

He wasn't a threat. Behind the alcohol, he was probably a nice enough guy. She was willing to give him the benefit of the doubt. That said, going anywhere with him wasn't on the menu. She brushed off his hand and was about to launch into a polite *well-hasn't-this-been-fun-but-I've-got-to-head-back-now-to-walk-the-dog* speech while simultaneously leaping to her feet and sprinting for the door, when she heard a voice behind her.

A dark, familiar voice that sent shivers racing up and down her spine.

She froze. Then slowly, very slowly, she turned around and there he was in all his ridiculously good-looking glory.

Four and a half wasted years and he still had the same effect on her. The man was six feet four inches of sexy, muscle-packed alpha male. Of Greek heritage, he had a burnished bronzed skin tone. His raven-black hair was just slightly too long, curling at the nape of his neck, and he had the classical features of a statue lovingly sculpted to perfection and then turned into living, breathing human form.

Right now, he was dressed in a pair of dark trousers that emphasised the length of his muscular legs and a white shirt cuffed to the elbows.

The crowded room, the mellow jazz and the bustle of people instantly dimmed to white background noise as Grace's eyes widened in alarm.

She was barely aware of Victor until she felt his hand on her arm and heard him say, with the over-enunciated precision of someone who's drunk too much, 'Friend of yours, Grace?'

Before Grace had time to answer that, Nico was dragging a third chair to the table and swinging it round so that he straddled it, arms resting loosely over the low back, his body language somehow oozing aggression.

Yet his expression was mild enough as his dark eyes swept over her companion and then stayed there.

'Oh, yes,' he purred. 'Grace and I are very good friends.'

'Nico…'

Grace was so disconcerted that she couldn't get beyond his name.

What on earth was Nico doing here? Shouldn't he have been on the other side of the Atlantic? In New York? Hadn't she booked his flight only a week ago, along with the usual five-star accommodation he demanded?

He was staring at Victor with undisguised curiosity and the sort of bone-deep insolence that needed no words to still feel like a threat.

Grace would have been furious but right now she was heady with relief.

Yes, she was absolutely fine when it came to dealing with most things, but she had dreaded the thought of having to deal with a drunk date.

'This is Victor,' she said crisply, while Nico continued to stare at Victor, who had fallen silent in the face of a more powerful and decidedly sober presence.

'Victor...'

'Nico, what are you doing here?'

'Same as you.' Nico shot her a quick look from under lush lashes. 'Having some fun. Except, when I spotted you from across the room, you didn't seem to be having a huge amount of that. Were you? Have I interrupted a fun time? If so, tell me and I'll leave immediately.'

He'd seen the way the man had shuffled his chair closer to hers, the way he'd tried to make inroads with his hands. He'd seen the way she'd politely pushed him back and revulsion had caught the back of his throat, as sour as bile.

The ferocity of his reaction had shocked him.

Since when had he ever been in the business of rescuing damsels in distress?

Nico had been twenty-three when he had last seriously rescued a damsel in distress, if you could call someone squatting next to an old jalopy with a flat tyre a damsel in distress. More a pocket-sized cute little thing who had known where to position that old jalopy of hers and who had stayed there in the certain knowledge that he would come along. That cute little thing had managed to steal his heart, or so he had thought before he'd wised up to the fact that the only thing she'd wanted to steal had been what was in his bank balance. When he'd tried to break up ten months after they'd met, by which time he'd recognised just how keen she'd been on all the material benefits he could bring to the table, she'd given him a piece of her mind and gone so far as to consult a lawyer to see if she could get anything on some spurious 'broken promises' platform.

Since then, Nico had learnt the wisdom of self-control so his utter lack of it when he had seen Grace from across the room confused the hell out of him.

'No answer?' He smiled a crocodile smile at Victor, who was now glaring accusingly at Grace.

Grace could see exactly what was going through his head and she was appalled. He'd insisted on paying for the two glasses of wine she'd had and for the tapas they'd shared. Had he thought that somehow that had entitled him to more than just dinner? Or had alcohol and perhaps nerves skewed his judgement? He'd gone from dull to insistent over the course of two and a half hours and he'd drunk an awful lot.

'Don't even think of outstaying your welcome,' Nico grated in a dangerously low voice. 'In fact, if I were you, I'd do the gentlemanly thing right now. I'd thank the lady for a terrific evening, wish her all the best and then head off into the sunset.'

'Nico…' Grace said again, mortified and suddenly overwhelmed with self-pity. Rescued by her boss. Wasn't that what it came down to? The very boss whose disturbing presence in her life was the reason she'd been here in the first place, trying to galvanise herself into doing what women of her age should be doing. Going out…meeting guys…dating and having fun.

Instead, Nico had spied her from across a crowded room and decided to turn into a knight in shining armour.

How on earth had it come to this?

But, of course, Grace knew, and as she pushed back the tears of self-pity she had a piercing flashback to her life, to the events that had determined the course of it.

She thought back to her mum, now on the other side of the world. Wasn't it, in some ways, because of her that she, Grace, was sitting here right now? Not quite knowing where to look, hating Nico for thinking he had to rescue her from an uncomfortable situation while reluctantly admiring him for the way he'd gone about doing it?

Cecily Brown, her mum, still young at forty-nine, was in Australia and on marriage number three. Cecily wasn't her real name. Her real name was Ann but, as she had once explained to a very young Grace, *Ann* was such a dreary name. How could an *Ann* be anything but dull? And Cecily had been very far from dull. Cecily had been a whirlwind of adventure, a gorgeous, gregarious red-haired beauty who had kicked out her first husband within three years of being married, only to see just sufficient of him over the remaining four years to get pregnant with another child before eventually divorcing him.

Somewhere along the line, she had married again, a marriage that had lasted a handful of months.

We all make mistakes. That had been her mother's casual dismissal of husband number two. Fortunately, the divorce had left her richer than she had been post-divorce number one, rich enough for her to pack in the nondescript office job she had spent years hating to follow the siren call of the stage.

And Cecily had followed that siren call with boundless enthusiasm. Young, vivacious and with not a scrap of common sense, she had enjoyed life in the manner of a single woman with zero responsibilities.

Parenting, for Cecily, had involved putting on little plays in the kitchen. There had been pizza for breakfast and cake for dinner and, of course, there had been days upon days with only the kindness of friends to keep her and her brother, five years her junior, fed.

Cecily had alternately proclaimed herself better off without men while going to pieces if she happened to be between boyfriends. There had been times when she had climbed into bed and stayed there for days on end with the curtains drawn while Grace had kept the home fires burning and then out she would come, in a blaze of boundless optimism, to pick up where she had left off.

Grace had witnessed all her mother's emotional highs and lows and every single one had determined the direction she wished her own life to take, and it wouldn't follow her mother's.

She had become independent from a young age and cautious beyond her years.

She had learnt that, while Cecily had been a fun mother, *fun* didn't go the distance when it came to parenting.

Parenting involved taking responsibility and Cecily had adroitly managed to delegate all responsibility to other people, largely Grace, who had never complained at the burden on her young shoulders.

So now?

She never took chances. Nico, with his revolving-door love life, was the very essence of a guy who only wanted to have fun, and the crush she'd had on him was inconvenient because he was the last person on earth she should be attracted to, never mind the small detail that he was her boss and paid her salary.

Her glamorous mother had needed validation from good-looking, eligible guys. She, Grace, did not and never would.

So, crush or no crush, she'd kept her distance except now, with Victor dispatched and Nico still sitting at the table, with the chair swivelled into its correct position, she had never felt more exposed.

His head was tilted to the side and his dark eyes were resting thoughtfully on her, ablaze with questions that were none of his business.

'What are you doing here?' Grace asked stiffly. 'Shouldn't you be in New York?'

'The guy bailed. His wife was rushed into hospital. Decided I'd spare myself a night in and come here instead.'

'On your own?'

She was gratified to see him flush and for a few seconds, he looked discomforted, which was rare for Nico Doukas.

'Actually, I came with someone.'

'Where is she?' Grace made a deal of looking around her, giving herself a chance to get her thoughts together, to distract herself from the horrendous awkwardness of the situation.

She'd put so much effort into making sure that there were clear boundaries between them.

Four and a half years of effort! Keeping her head firmly screwed on whenever he was around!

It had been vital because Nico knew how to make a woman feel special. He did it without even realising it. Perched on the side of her desk, he could be chatting about spreadsheets and stationery supplies and he *still* always managed to make her feel as though every word that left her mouth by way of response were a fascinating revelation.

God only knew what he must be like in the company of women he was actively trying to impress.

The fact that she secretly lusted after the man had made it all the more important that she erect her barriers and remain well behind them.

It was galling to think that in a heartbeat and through some cruel twist of fate all that effort could be reduced to rubble.

'I didn't think there was much point in her hanging around while I came…over here…'

'There was no need to ruin your evening by rushing over here to rescue me.' Grace straightened in the chair but even as she did so, even as she tried to revert to her usual crisp, businesslike manner, she was conscious of the frivolity of her dress, all froth and flowers and straps.

It was hot outside, a rare, picture-perfect August evening, and she had dressed to impress.

At five ten and slender, she lacked boobs and curves but made a good enough clothes horse and she had gone all out to play up her assets, such as they were.

'You…looked…' Nico shook his head and the flush darkened, delineating his sharp cheekbones and making him look suddenly younger than his thirty-five years '…as though the man was making you uncomfortable. Even from a distance I could tell he'd had too much to drink…'

'And you figured that I might not have been able to handle the situation?' Grace enquired tartly, yet when she thought of him getting rid of his date so that he could come to her rescue, something hot inside her flared into unwelcome life.

She felt the pinch of her nipples grazing against her bra and wetness between her legs made her want to squirm.

He'd seen her and flown over…come to save her

from the fool she'd ended up with who'd started to make her feel uncomfortable... It wasn't a compliment, was it? But whatever it was, it made her achingly conscious of him in ways that felt, oh, so dangerous right now...

When she next spoke, her voice was sharper than she'd intended. 'Nico, I can take care of myself.'

'Yes, I realise that but...'

'But what?' She clicked her tongue, eager to re-establish herself as the efficient employee who was never flustered and could deal with anything. 'I'm very capable of dealing with...with anything. You should know that! How many times have you given me an impossible task only to find that I deal with it in record time? You've said that yourself so many times! I don't need anyone to feel sorry for me and I definitely didn't need you to cancel your plans for the evening because you felt you had to save me from my date.'

'Did I mention anything about feeling sorry for you?'

Nico raked restless fingers through his dark hair. In truth he had rushed over here without thought. He had seen her, had felt something shift inside him, something weird and oddly powerful, like a rush of air racing past him, blowing through him and leaving before he had time to bottle it and find out what it was.

She'd worked for him for over four years. He had

seen more of her than most men saw of their wives and yet the sight of her here, in this sultry, atmospheric jazz club, shorn of her usual starchy trappings, had kick-started something inside him he hadn't been able to put a finger on.

And when he'd realised that the guy she was with was being a pest…when he'd seen the way she'd shoved his hand aside, polite and firm but with just a hint of anxiety, he hadn't stopped to think twice.

He'd dismissed his date without a backward glance and flown over like just the sort of damned rescuer she certainly hadn't asked for and didn't want.

As she was now taking great pains to inform him.

Nico refused to question why, exactly, he had felt so compelled to fly to her side.

Nor was he going to delve deep into his shock at seeing her looking the way she looked now, still cool and remote but with a sizzle of sexual allure that he hadn't previously realised was there.

Or had he?

He brushed aside that tantalising thought while refusing to apologise for being the perfect gentleman in coming to her aid. Even if she hadn't asked for it.

'And yes,' he grated, 'you are up to pretty much anything I can throw at you in the work environment, but we're not in a work environment now, and my apologies if I was out of order in thinking that that man you were with might have been making you feel a bit uncomfortable. Was he? By the way? Because you didn't seem too gutted when I got rid of him.'

Grace sighed.

He'd done his good deed for the day. So what if she wished the ground could open and swallow her up because the last thing she needed was for her sexy boss to see her as someone he felt sorry for?

Sure, not when it came to work, but here? In a club? For him, a different matter.

Here, away from the familiar stamping ground where he knew her for what she was, his reliable, efficient secretary, she was out of her depth. He had spotted that from across the room and had stormed over because he'd assumed she was in a situation she couldn't handle.

She was thirty-one years old and he knew her well enough to know that, underneath the official trappings, she wasn't a woman who was used to the ways of the world. She wasn't a woman like the ones he dated.

It made her teeth snap together with frustration but what could she do?

The more she protested and fought against his act of chivalry, the more bewildered he would become at her overreaction.

He wasn't going to politely step aside and leave her be. He was a guy who had no objections to being a bull in a china shop if the occasion demanded, and since when were bulls in china shops interested in polite behaviour?

Nico was curious and she couldn't blame him. She'd made such a big deal of being private that of course he was going to be curious in a situation like this.

'Victor was…becoming a bit of a nuisance,' she admitted. 'It's the first time we've gone out on a date and I had no idea he would end up drinking so much that he…'

Grace fiddled with the stem of her wine glass and her eyes skittered away from his piercing stare.

'Some people can't hold their drink,' Nico rasped. 'One too many and the inner creep takes over. Did he do anything more than just make you feel uncomfortable? Did he try and…touch you?'

'No!' But she laughed. 'Why? Would you offer to go and pummel him on my behalf?'

'Damn right.'

'You're kidding, Nico.' Their eyes tangled and there was a brief, breathless silence. Her pulses leapt and, for a few seconds, every thought was driven from her head because there was a burning intensity in his dark eyes that made her feel giddy and sharply alert at the same time.

'I don't joke about certain things.'

'Well, he didn't. He was just a bore and then a pest. That's all.' He was still looking at her in a way that made her blood sizzle and she rushed into chatter, which was so unlike her. She confessed that he was an Internet date and then launched into a nonsensical monologue about dating apps, growing redder and more flustered by the second. Eventually she lapsed into embarrassed silence, mortified and despairing at how utterly she had let herself down.

'The Internet can be a dangerous place, especially for a beautiful woman.'

Grace's eyes widened. She wondered whether, in her feverish panic at the way the conversation was going, she had imagined what she'd heard. Maybe she'd been hallucinating, having some kind of out-of-body experience.

But then he reached out and covered her hand with his. His eyes didn't leave her face. Just that hand, warm on hers, idly stroking...

And her body went up in flames. They licked past all the defences she had erected over the years, sweeping them under a blast of heat as scorching as a furnace. Her heart was a drumbeat that made her feel sick and faint. She was trembling and her breathing had slowed as her body responded to his casual touch.

It was as if she had been fast asleep and now, eyes wide open, life was rushing at her in dazzling, Technicolour fury.

It was terrifying and she snatched her hand away and rubbed it, lost for words.

'I... I think I'll be heading home now,' she

breathed jerkily, and Nico sprawled back in his chair.

'Let me get my driver to take you.'

'No! No... I... I can make my own way back.' His voice was its usual lazy drawl while she had to clear her throat to avoid sounding like someone with a speech impediment. 'Monday,' she gabbled, standing and snatching at her bag, at once eager to leave but conscious of the floaty summer dress and her body on fire under it.

'Monday?'

'I'll have those reports for you first thing! I've also...also done some checking up on the security systems at Deals, making sure there are no viruses in the system before I start loading sensitive information.'

'Grace,' Nico said softly, 'I'm sorry your evening didn't work out the way you wanted it to. Head home, sleep it off and don't even dare think about anything work related until you're in on Monday. Nothing is so important that you need to log onto your work computer on a weekend.'

He slapped his thighs and stood as well, towering over her, emanating waves of heat that furled around her like a miasma and scrambled her thoughts.

'Have a good weekend...whatever's left of it...' He saluted her with a half-smile on his face. 'And word to the wise...be careful on those dating sites. You never know what or who you're going to find there.'

'Thanks for the advice, Nico,' Grace countered sweetly. 'I'll bear that in mind the next time I venture out into the big, bad world.'

And before he could say anything else on the subject, she spun round on her heel and walked away.

CHAPTER TWO

FOR THE FIRST time in years, Grace approached the glass and steel building where she worked with trepidation.

She had left the bar two evenings before on the verge of a nervous breakdown. Only on the bus back to her apartment had she got her thoughts in order enough to reflect on just how much Nico had managed to kick ajar the door that had always been closed between them, and all because of a chance encounter, and, wow, had he kicked that door in grand style.

She'd felt like a swooning Victorian maiden when he'd put that hand on hers, softly stroking…his eyes fastened to her face, dragging responses out of her she'd been so careful to hide.

Would her charming, charismatic and way too sexy boss suddenly decide that if a couple of barriers had been broken down, then why not have a go at knocking down the whole edifice? When she had first started working for him, she could remember the way he would look at her, with those dark, slumberous eyes coolly speculating, wondering what lay beneath the controlled, calm façade. He did that sort of thing without even realising it. She was sure of it. It was all part and parcel of his magnetic personality. He was the son of a Greek shipping tycoon and he would have grown up with the sort of bone-deep confidence that came so naturally to people born into wealth, a casual assumption that wherever their interest happened to alight, the recipient of said interest would be flattered to death.

Grace was honest enough to admit to herself that she would find it difficult if he suddenly decided to infiltrate her private life. She didn't want the lines between them to be trampled. She couldn't let her barriers down with him. She was far too aware of her boss as *a man* and one whose casual approach to relationships she found personally distasteful.

Yes, he was the smartest guy she had ever met. Yes, he treated his staff fairly and was generous to a fault when it came to paying them. And yes, she had seen enough of his business practices to know that he played it straight down the line without taking any of the sort of financial shortcuts she knew some business tycoons were guilty of doing.

But he played the field and he did it without any trace of a conscience. Grace had grown up alert to the dangers of people who played the field, who moved on from one relationship to another without stopping to work out what the collateral damage might be. Between marriages, her mother had seldom been on her own, without a guy. Caught on a treadmill of always needing to be needed, always looking for distraction, she had been a part-time parent, even after Tommy had had his accident and had needed her to be a full-time mother. At least for a while. She was vivacious and beautiful and vain and fun, but she had never realised that there was more to life than that when it came to the people around her. Grace had realised because, after Tommy's accident had put him in a coma and then, when he had surfaced, confined him to a wheelchair, she had been the one to do the coping and it had been agonising.

Grace never uttered a word when Nico asked her to order expensive flowers to mark the end of a relationship and she showed no emotion when, a handful of days later, she was on the phone reserving seats at the theatre for his next conquest.

But that love 'em and leave 'em attitude? That ability to take like a kid in a sweet shop and then move on when the sweets got boring? No, those were traits she had no time for. Even her mother had at least moved in and out of men in search of Mr Right. Nico moved in and out of women because he was committed to having a good time.

Yet still her disobedient eyes surreptitiously followed him as he moved with lazy grace in his office, walking and thinking aloud while she did her best to keep up with the lightning speed of his thoughts… and her disobedient mind? It bypassed common sense to have fun with all sorts of taboo thoughts and images that made her quiver when she lay in bed at night, waiting for sleep to get a grip.

In an attempt to bolster her defences, she had chosen a particularly uninspiring outfit to wear. A tweedy grey knee-length skirt, a white blouse neatly tucked into the waistband of the skirt, tights and flat black pumps. She had dragged her hair behind her ears to clip severely into place and, with her laptop bag in one hand and her handbag in the other, she looked and felt as carefree as a teacher employed to keep order in a class of rebellious teenagers.

Of course, he was there before her even though it wasn't yet eight-thirty. She stopped only to dump the handbag, remove her laptop from its bag and was already flipping it open as she strode into his office, briefly knocking to announce her arrival.

She didn't look at him.

She *couldn't*.

And yet, she *still* managed to note that he was in a pair of pale grey trousers and a striped shirt that was cuffed to the elbows and with the top couple of buttons undone, revealing just enough of a hard sliver of brown chest to send her imagination whirring in heated response. She was used to this sort of nonsensical reaction…indeed, it was one of the very reasons she had decided to try her hand at Internet dating, because she finally accepted just how much she needed to remind herself that the world was full of other guys and not just this one unsuitable one. That said, she was hypersensitive to every nuanced heated response racing through her now because of what had happened. For a moment in time, she hadn't been his secretary. She had been a woman without the suit and the computer, for once not transcribing emails or arranging his appointments or discussing whatever deals he had in the melting pot. She had been a woman in a slinky flowered dress on a date.

'I've collated all those emails,' she said, automatically sitting in her usual spot on the chair in front of his desk and peering at her computer, 'on the supplies issue with the freight ship from South America. I can send them off to the lawyer at your say-so? Also…' brow furrowed, she continued without break '…Christopher Thomas wants you to call him urgently about the takeover of his company. He says he wants to add some further clauses about maintaining staff levels for a certain length of time. Shall I set up a conference call? I've checked your diary and you have a slot between two and three-thirty this afternoon but only if we can shift your overseas call to Australia by half an hour.'

She finally risked looking at him and their eyes met.

'And breathe…' Nico murmured.

Grace pursed her lips. 'I have a huge amount to get through today. I thought I'd get the ball rolling because I… I have to leave early this afternoon, I'm afraid…'

'How early?' Nico frowned.

'Three-thirty. I have a dental appointment. I'm

sorry. I should have texted you to let you know this morning, but a free slot's only just come up on my way in...'

She didn't have an appointment. Nerves had got the better of her and it was infuriating because it was the first time it had happened. Her quiet, predictable world had shifted on its axis and now she felt as though she had to get it back to where it had been as fast as possible, and being here all day, dealing with Nico and that alarming inquisitive glitter in his dark eyes, wasn't going to help matters.

'It's crucial that we take care of our teeth,' Nico murmured by way of response.

He stood up, unconsciously flexing his muscles before strolling to the floor-to-ceiling glass pane to briefly peer out before turning to look at her.

Grace reluctantly looked at him. She refused to rise to the bait. She intended to do her utmost to move on from what had happened in the jazz club but she could tell from the gleam in his dark eyes that her boss might not be that interested in playing ball.

'So shall we get down to work, Nico?' she asked coolly. 'I know you'd probably like nothing more than to talk about...what happened...but I would really rather not discuss it. It was unfortunate that you showed up when I was there with...with Victor, but these things happen. Best we put all that nonsense behind us.' There. She'd faced down the elephant in the room because it was pointless trying to tiptoe around it and pretend it didn't exist.

* * *

Her gaze held his, as calm and cool as always, but it wasn't hard for Nico to spot the simmering defiance there. She had come, he'd realised just as soon as she had walked through that door, with all her defences back in place. Outside the sun was already warning of another hot, unbearably sticky day and yet here she was in her best protective gear.

Previously, Nico would have been amused, but things had changed and he was frustrated at just how determined she was to pretend it was all back to business and let's forget about that blip. He was even more frustrated at just how keen he was to fight against that, as though now that he had happened to find his foot wedged in the door, he wanted to kick open the door and discover what lay beyond it.

Why? What had changed so much? He had re-treated successfully for years from trying to prod and poke a response from her, intrigued against his will by a woman who was so immune to him. He had backed away and settled into a routine of working with someone who'd shaped up to be the best PA he'd ever had. He'd told himself that curiosity was not worth the hassle of having to source someone com-parable because he had ignored her *Hands Off* signs.

But now…

Who could blame a guy for having a curious streak? Curiosity had got him where he was today. Sure, he had inherited the family empire and, with that, all the kudos and wealth that came with it. He could have stuck to what he knew and carried on the shipping tradition. Lord knew, his own father had had his work cut out when he had been forced to steer it into safe waters after his brother's reckless handling of the asset base. So it should have been in his nature not to take risks, but he had because there were other worlds out there to be explored and shipping was just one of them.

If he hadn't been curious enough to have a look and then to have a go, he would have remained in Athens to take over the reins of the family business. He would have followed in his father's footsteps. He would have had his youthful drama, learnt his lessons and then married a good Greek girl, just as his father had, and stayed put to toe the family line.

He had wanted more than that and he had explored and mastered so many fields in technology and communication that staying close to home had never been an option. He had made sure that the family business was in robust health, but he had moved on. His own private companies were worth their own individual fortunes.

So curious? It was in his DNA and his efficient and dependable secretary roused all kinds of curiosity inside him. He was hanging onto common sense by a thread but when he thought of her in that dress and the way it cupped her high, small breasts…his libido took off at supersonic speed.

Nico could enjoy the novelty of it, could be tempted by thoughts of going beyond what common sense was dictating and yet know, in his gut, that those temptations were indulgences he would be very wise not to explore. He'd had his brush with adventure. He'd been a fool once, had taken his eye off the ball, and it wasn't going to happen again. Fun was temporary. He would eventually marry and that would be to a suitable woman, one whose status equalled his and who came from a tradition of work first.

Inappropriate thoughts about his secretary made him uneasy because it was outside known territory. He enjoyed the company of women, treated them like queens and was utterly monogamous, but he always let them know what they could and couldn't expect from him. Boundary lines were always in place. *That* was known territory. Sudden idle thoughts about his secretary were not.

He sauntered thoughtfully back to his desk and, when he sat back down, he pushed the chair back at an angle and leaned back, hands folded behind his head, and looked at her for a few seconds.

'Let's forget about work for ten minutes, Grace,' he said quietly. 'I know you want to pretend that Saturday night never happened, but it did.'

'I don't want to *pretend* anything, Nico.'

'When I got to that club and spotted you, I was shocked.'

'I don't know why, Nico. Believe it or not, I do actually have a life that happens when I leave this office.'

'I'm not disputing that, but it's been hard to envisage because you've spent the past four and a half years making sure you never breathed a word to me about what you do when you leave here.'

'Because it's none of your business!'

'You're my business, because you work for me and because I'd like to think that we're a bit more than a couple of strangers who happen to be together because of work.'

Nico watched her fidget. He noted the hectic colour in her cheeks. He'd shocked himself when he'd flown to her rescue two days before and he was astonished that he was now pursuing this in the face of common sense telling him that detachment was what he did best.

'I was worried on your behalf, Grace.'

'And like I said, there was no need to be!'

'Because you can look after yourself?'

'That's right.'

Nico looked at her coolly defiant face—so remote and so oddly alluring. Was he only noticing this for the first time or was it something he had unconsciously noted all along but had chosen to ignore until he had seen her in a different light?

'Look—' Grace leapt to her feet, her cheeks flushed '—let's get something straight, Nico. I made it clear when I joined your company, when I started working for you, that I wasn't interested in putting my private life in the public arena. Nothing's changed on that front.'

'We have very different definitions of private life

in the public arena,' Nico returned with a thread of amusement. 'And sit back down, for God's sake. You're not being cross-examined in the witness box with the threat of jail if you don't supply the correct answers. We're having a conversation.' He looked at her with brooding intensity. Every bit of her screamed discomfort. He'd never seen her so agitated in his life before but, then again, he concluded that he'd only ever seen the parts of her she had been willing to put on show. Under that smooth, composed exterior, there obviously lurked a complex, fiery woman.

Grace sat back down.

She was rattled. How to play this? What to do? How far could she insist on being secretive without him wondering why? How long before he began to wonder whether she singled him out because she wasn't relaxed around him? And once he started asking himself questions like that, how long before he found his unexpected answers? That he got under her skin? That she was attracted to him?

'I'm not hiding anything,' she said reluctantly. She raised her eyes to his and forced herself to relax. Also to accept that digging her heels in was only going to make him more and more curious about her. She couldn't kid herself that bumping into him in the most unlikely of venues wasn't going to make him curious, and the more she tried to stuff the genie back in the bottle, the more curious he was going to become. Human nature.

But caution was so deeply ingrained that she didn't know where to begin when it came to sharing, least of all with Nico, and the silence stretched between them.

'Grace…' Nico eventually broke the silence, raking his fingers through his dark hair in a gesture that was both elegant and sexy and one that she was accustomed to seeing because he did it often. 'Okay.' He sighed. 'I get it that you and I are on a different page when it comes to being upfront. I get it that you're tight-lipped on every single aspect of your private life, for reasons that are frankly mystifying, but you work for me, have worked for me for a very long time, and I like to think that we're…we're *friends*. Wouldn't you agree?'

'Yes!' Grace thought of all those forbidden thoughts over the years. None could be described as in the *friendly* category. 'Of course we are. Of course I consider you my friend as well as my boss. Good heavens, we see enough of one another!'

'I'm glad you agree! Which is why I felt compelled to join you on Saturday. Naturally I would never have intruded had I not got the distinct impression that the man was bugging you. And it's because I care about your welfare that I felt the need to offer you advice rather than sit back and watch you wander into situations that you may find you can't handle.'

Grace gritted her teeth in something resembling a smile. So they were here again, were they?

'You need to be careful. You put yourself out there and…' he shook his head '…you have no idea what could be lurking around the corner. That date of yours? Sure, he'd had too much to drink and maybe he's a paragon of virtue when he's sober, but under the influence of drink you can never be certain what direction a guy might take if he's rejected. There can be a thin line between thinking you're in control of a situation as a woman and realising that you're not.'

'Yes, you said something of the sort when you… came to my rescue two evenings ago,' Grace said sweetly, while she counted to ten and then to twenty, making sure to keep her temper in check.

Nico frowned.

'So we agree…' he murmured.

'Not really, because I don't tell *you* how to run *your* life.'

Lush, silky lashes shielded Nico's expression for a couple of seconds but there was a lazy smile on his face when he drawled, softly, 'Would you like to?'

'That's not my place,' Grace countered quickly. His dark eyes on her made her skin prickle and she licked her lips. She could feel the pulse in her neck beating fast.

She longed for the safety of her desk and her computer and emails that needed urgent attention. And yet, just as when he had surprised her at that jazz club, there was a simmering, dangerous excitement inside her. For someone who had always led a cautious life, never taking chances, it was heady and disturbing and frightening.

So why did she like it?

'We're friends,' Nico encouraged smoothly.

'Yes, but there's also a lot of work to get through…'

'This is more important,' Nico said firmly. 'Seeing you in such a state of panic on Saturday evening—'

'I was not in a state of panic!' Grace interrupted impatiently.

'Perhaps that's a slight exaggeration.'

'I was uncomfortable. Not the end of the world.'

'As I was saying, Grace, seeing you in such discomfort made me realise that you're more than just someone I pay to come in between the hours of nine to five to work for me…' He shifted but kept his eyes pinned to her face. 'You're someone I care about and it's because I care about you that I want these barriers between us to drop. I want you to feel free to express yourself around me, to tell me what's on your mind…' He gestured to their surroundings, which were the last word in plush. 'If I don't know what you think, then how do I know whether you're enjoying your job or not?'

Grace looked at her boss and the sincere expression on his face with frustration.

Had she been the only one to feel that sizzle of something when his hand had covered hers? She had been secretly thrilled that he had rushed to her side in the club even though she might noisily make her stand for independence. It irked her that she couldn't shake all those feelings of attraction, that she couldn't get onto the same page as Nico and see the sudden shift between them as a friendship that would simply mark a different chapter in their relationship.

She was desperate for everything to remain *work only* within the glass walls of his expensive offices.

Anything beyond that scared her because she wasn't sure how she could handle it. Fancying him made her vulnerable and she didn't want to be vulnerable.

She'd been vulnerable as a kid and she wasn't going to revisit that place again.

'I love my job.'

'But what about the guy who gave it to you? Hmm?' He grinned with wicked amusement. 'Less love there?'

'You're playing games.'

'Maybe a little,' Nico admitted, 'but it's true that we've taken a step forward and it's important we keep it where it is because I'm genuinely interested in knowing what you think about me, aside from what you think about the job or the offices or the pay cheque at the end of the month. A happy employee is a loyal employee and if you have any problems with me, then I want you to take this opportunity to air them…'

Grace relaxed and fumbled her way to ground she could understand. Nico, for all his charm, thought with his head. Was he protecting his asset? He valued her professionalism and over the years she had had her salary increased hugely along with her responsibilities.

After four and a half years of seeing only one side of her, was he suddenly keen to make sure there was nothing she was hiding from him that might jeopardise their very successful working arrangement?

Had seeing her with Victor made him realise how little he knew her and therefore how easily she could pull the rug from under his feet by letting him down on the work front because she wasn't happy about telling him what she thought? What she really thought? He suspected that she didn't approve of his colourful love life, as he'd said himself, in passing.

But where he had maybe given it no thought, had he now woken up to the fact that the woman he now realised he didn't know half as well as he'd thought might just be banking her disapproval? Quietly biding her time until the scales overbalanced and she took off for another job?

Nothing mattered more to Nico than work. It was the one thing on which he was deadly focused.

As if to confirm what she was thinking, he said, in low voice, 'Be honest with me, Grace. I value you and if you're storing things up…well, that's a recipe for disaster. You're the best PA I've ever had. I don't want you to suddenly quit on me because…you have issues with me…' He shot her one of those devastating smiles that could make her melt from the inside out. One of those smiles that, in the past, had made her tingle with warmth on the inside even though, on the outside, she had always been able to remain perfectly composed. Unfortunately, because she was fighting for composure, that smile made her feel horribly exposed and vulnerable.

And the twinkle in his dark eyes riled her because she could sense just the tiniest bit of mischief there, however sincere he might be. He'd crossed no boundaries for so long that he was having fun stomping all over them now.

So he wanted her to be honest? Well, why not?

Maybe, in fact, it would dilute this crazy spell he seemed to have over her. Who was to say that all these cloak and dagger, childish yearnings didn't contribute to her ill-advised crush? Didn't clandestine relationships flourish in the thrill of secrecy only to fizzle out the minute they were subjected to the glare of tedious, out-in-the-open reality?

It might be her nature to guard her personal life, purely from habit, but if she opened up a bit, then whatever curiosity Nico might be nurturing about her because he had happened to see her out of context would be killed dead in its tracks.

She would become what he was accustomed to. He had the sort of lively mind that enjoyed pushing the boundaries. If she had suddenly become one of those boundaries he might be interested in pushing, then getting their working relationship onto a slightly more normalised footing might not be such a bad thing.

If he wanted to invite her to ask questions, then why shouldn't she?

She harked back to what he had said and picked up the thread.

'I don't tell you how to run your life, Nico, but now you're asking, I really disapprove of the way you treat women.'

'The way *I treat women*? You mean with frankness, generosity and consideration? *That* way?'

'You break hearts. I know that. I've dealt with those weeping broken hearts down the end of the telephone.'

'I'm always honest. You couldn't find a more honest guy than me. Women always know the score from the very beginning. Nothing long term. Nothing permanent. But while it lasts, they become my sole preoccupation and I am lavish when it comes to spending on them.'

'They know the score?' Grace's eyebrows shot up. 'There aren't many women who start going out with a guy knowing that it isn't going anywhere... no woman is a mind-reader.'

'Then that's not my fault because I'm very truthful with all of them. I lay my cards on the table and tell it like it is.'

'Do you? Literally?'

'I don't like misunderstandings so I spell it all out in no uncertain terms from the get-go. No cosy meals in…no holding hands in front of the telly in the evening…no meeting the parents…no chats about future plans and no idly gazing into jewellery stores and musing about the joys of family life… In fact, not even sleepovers. I like my space to myself.'

Bombarded by the sort of unequivocal information she had always suspected but never had confirmed, Grace could only look at Nico with her mouth half open and he burst out laughing and held her astonished gaze for a few seconds longer than necessary.

'Okay, maybe it's not quite as bold as that, but I always tell them that I'm not interested in anything long term and they get the message on the rest pretty soon afterwards.'

'But why?'

'But why what?' Nico frowned.

'I mean…' She turned bright red as she realised that the question-and-answer session was in danger of overstepping its brief.

'You mean,' Nico said coolly, 'why I'm not interested in chasing after happy-ever-after scenarios?'

'Most people do want to find love…a companion…a soulmate, if you will…'

'Is that *your* aim? Was that what you were looking for when you decided to go with that Internet guy?'

Grace tilted her chin at a defensive angle. She didn't want to be reminded of that mistake but, then again, wasn't it better to be hopeful of finding love than to accept that it was never going to happen?

She might approach life from a different direction than her mother had, but, in the end, weren't their aims similar?

Of course, there was no way she would ever be prepared to kiss a thousand frogs on her way to finding her prince, as her mother had been prepared to do, but hadn't her mother at least had that goal in sight? And she had found that prince.

If you never had that goal to aim for, then surely life would be a little empty?

If Nico was curious about her, Grace was honest enough to admit that it was mutual.

But this curiosity? It had to be leashed. She knew that. Yet, she wondered what had informed his choices and she was so desperate to ask that she had to clamp shut her jaw.

'I wasn't looking for anything,' she said. 'Just some fun.'

Nico's dark gaze rested speculatively on her fine-featured face. Did he believe her? No. Not really. She was a serious woman who wanted more than just a bit of fun.

Was Internet date number one the beginning of that search?

Nico lowered his eyes. Images rushed into his head of her with a man, finding true love. He'd been goading her. Just a little bit. Just to see the tinge of pink in her cheeks, spurred on by who knew what?

But now, when he thought of his serious secretary in the arms of whatever soulmate she was looking for, he felt something tight and uncomfortable in his belly.

A woman in love was an unreliable employee, he grittily told himself, banking down a little voice that wanted to whisper different things in his ear. *That* was why he was suddenly disconcerted at the turn of the conversation.

'So,' he drawled, 'shall we wrap up this soul-searching for the moment and do what we do best?'

It took Grace a few disoriented seconds before her work hat was back in place as she registered his brisk change of tone and she nodded.

'Back to work.' She smiled and stood up and brushed some non-existent dust from her skirt and flashed him a smile.

'You have a dentist appointment, after all,' he murmured.

'So I do.' She'd completely forgotten. For the past forty minutes, she'd completely forgotten far too much.

CHAPTER THREE

NICO TERMINATED THE forty-five-minute phone call with his father in Greece and sprang from where he'd been relaxing in his sprawling sitting room to prowl to the kitchen for a drink. He needed it. Something very strong to deal with what had been thrown at him out of the blue.

'It is your uncle, Nico,' his father had said heavily, after the briefest of pleasantries. 'You do not know it, but he has been ill for some time. I have had news of his death. Arrangements will have to be made, son. I, myself, would go but you know your mother is still recovering from her operation last month. I am in no position to leave her and the process should only take a few days. I am relying on you to step in on my behalf.'

Now, Nico poured himself a glass of whisky and mused that this was not what he had had in mind when he had decided to head back to his place for one of his rare evenings in on his own. It was Friday, it was only just a little after six and he had planned on kicking back in front of a complex computer program that had been submitted from the small, innovative logistics company he had recently bought. Peace. And a chance for his head to be somewhere else because, for the past three weeks, far too much of it had been taken up with his secretary and her sudden irresistible appeal.

Curiosity was proving annoyingly immune to all the usual stun-gun weapons in his armoury. Things had settled back to where they had once been, before that blip. She was once again the dutiful, highly professional secretary who dealt with whatever was thrown at her without complaint and with praiseworthy efficiency.

If he had imagined that their first truly honest conversation might have opened a door that would stay ajar, then he had found himself to be completely mistaken.

She might have been slightly more forthcoming when he'd asked her how her weekend had been… or what she thought of this or that piece of gossip in the news…or, daringly, whether there had been any more Internet hopefuls on the scene…but the polite *hands off* mask was firmly back in place. As were the suits and the neatly tied-back hair and the lowered eyes as she sat in front of him, her fingers flying over her laptop, doing what she did so well. Working.

Nothing wrong with that, Nico repeatedly told himself. He needed a calm, stress-free working environment and she had always provided that and was continuing to do so now.

He hadn't been exaggerating when he'd told her that she was the best PA he'd ever had. Previous to her, he had endured the nightmare of three too young and too easily panicked secretaries, one harridan with only a passing acquaintance with the software he needed her to know and one efficient older woman who had dramatically had to leave after six months because her daughter in Scotland had had triplets and had wanted her to be on hand to help.

Grace had shown up for the interview and within minutes Nico had known that he was going to hire her.

So he was frustrated and impatient with himself for his sudden lack of self-control now whenever he was around her.

And on the back of that phone call? Well, it was no good trying to while away a couple of pleasant hours playing with all the mathematical intricacies of the computer program, trying to improve some of the complex coding, which would have guaranteed total preoccupation with something else.

His uncle.

A blast from the past.

Nico nursed the whisky and thought about the implications of heading off to a tiny island in the Bahamas for what might be longer than the optimistic couple of days his father had opined, in order to wrap up his uncle's affairs.

Sander Doukas, the disgraced black sheep of the family, was a shadowy figure who had never featured in Nico's life, except anecdotally.

He had brought disgrace on the family name. Photos of him in compromising situations had been so numerous that you could wallpaper a house with the cuttings. He had been in rehab three times. He practically had a loyalty card there.

That was the gossip Nico had gleaned from a variety of sources.

What Nico *did* know for certain was that Sander Doukas had come so close to running the family company into the ground that the ensuing battle for power between his father and his uncle had destroyed whatever family bond they had once shared.

They had shared the inheritance of the company when their parents had suddenly and unexpectedly been killed in a car accident. Sander had been, by then, a lightweight member of the board, rarely seen and largely overlooked. He had been thirty and far too busy having fun to don a suit and go to work.

Five years younger, Stefano Doukas, Nico's father, had already been learning the ropes and proving himself to be as serious as Sander had been frivolous.

Had a substantial inheritance not landed on Sander's shoulders at a young age, Nico assumed all would have continued relatively smoothly because the old man, his grandfather and the head of the company, would have kept his older son on a short lead. However, that wasn't to be.

Through the years, Nico had come to realise just how destructive it was to have no control over your emotional life. He had been young but not so young that he hadn't understood those hushed conversations between his parents and the comings and goings of lawyers as power had eventually been wrested away from Sander, with many concessions to sweeten the blow.

In all events, the upshot had been banishment in all but name.

The banishment had been suitably luxurious. Sander had been sent to open and run a hotel on an exquisite island of the Bahamas in the Caribbean.

'Does he keep in touch?' he could remember asking his father many years previously.

To which his father had shaken his head and said, without emotion, 'Too much pride. So be it. We all get the life that we deserve in the end. Left to his own devices, your uncle would have destroyed the company, and the company, my son, was not founded to support a spoiled man's indulgences. Many people's lives depend on it. Have fun, but it is important to know when the fun has to stop.'

Nico had had no curiosity about an uncle he had never known. It was unthinkable that he would refuse his father's request, but it was still annoying, he thought as he drained the last of the whisky in his glass, because he had a lot on his plate at the moment and wrapping up affairs had an ominous ring about it.

On a small island in the middle of nowhere, who knew how long the procedure would take?

He would have to carry on working.

He assumed all mod cons would be in place, although he had no idea what sort of hotel his uncle had set up. He had been shuffled out of harm's way, with sufficient money to last more than a lifetime but doled out by a trusted, designated member of the company, and then left to his own devices.

Arrangements would have to be made now and urgently.

Nico realised that he had no idea where Grace lived because he'd never had cause to go to her house.

He wouldn't spring a surprise visit on her now, at any rate, even if he did know where she lived.

On the other hand, he couldn't sit around waiting until Monday. Like it or not, she was about to have her weekend disrupted…

Grace had not been expecting a call from her boss.

Were things back to normal between them? Not for her. For her, the memory of his hand moving softly over hers was still too vivid. She closed her eyes and could relive the sensation. So when he had disappeared early this afternoon, she had been surprised but not displeased.

It was a Friday and she'd decided that she would relax over the weekend, visit her brother as she always did on a Sunday, and then on Monday she would kick-start the dating site and take her chances again. Did lightning strike twice?

So his name popping up on her phone jolted her. It was a little after seven and, even though she was very happy to be doing nothing, Grace possessed sufficient self-awareness to feel a twinge of embarrassment that she wasn't out having fun.

How had *having fun* ended up on a par with *surviving an ordeal*? When had *having fun* entailed gritting her teeth and girding her loins and taking lots of deep breaths before going for it?

'Nico?'

'Glad I caught you, Grace.'

His disembodied voice sent a little shiver through her.

'Is anything wrong?' This could only be about work and now she frantically tried to think if she'd left something unfinished. For a few pleasurable seconds, she was seduced into fantasising that he was calling her to ask her out. She half closed her eyes and got a grip. She'd wasted too many years on fantasies like this and she'd reached the end of the line with that.

'I did stay on after you left, Nico, and got through as much as I could. If there's something I should have done, then tell me and I can fit it in over the weekend.'

'Fit work in over the weekend?'

'Yes, of course.'

'You're not paid to fit work in over the weekend.'

'I know, but—'

'Besides, haven't you got plans?'

'Well, yes. I'm busy on Sunday…' Grace thought of Tommy, of how much he needed her, how much he had *always* needed her. Sundays were their day. She was always there for him, egging him on, encouraging him, always keen to try and see what more she could do to make his life a little easier.

Whatever foolish confidences she had shared with Nico, that was one she never would, that was a very private side to her that would not be in the public domain.

'Internet date?'

'Nico, why have you called? Is it about work?'

'Yes and no. I need to have a word with you. I wouldn't have interrupted your Friday evening, Grace, but this can't wait. I need to see you. We can do this one of three ways. I can either come to your house, you can come to mine or we can meet at the office. It should be busy there at the moment. There's a social event happening several floors down, some art exhibition McGregor's giving to try and impress the great and the good in culture, and my people will also be burning the midnight oil working on that computer program I want them to perfect by Monday.'

'You're making me nervous, Nico. Can't you tell me what this is about?'

Come to her house? Grace could think of nothing she wanted less. Nico had never been to her house.

There had never been any reason for him to come and even if something urgent had cropped up, she would have done her best to make sure he didn't put one foot over her threshold. Perhaps, even, one foot in the street where she lived or even the town, for that matter, because she knew that he would have been shocked.

Shocked that she didn't live in a smart apartment in a smart part of town, because she was certainly paid enough to afford somewhere really nice. He would have wondered where her very fat pay cheque went. He would never know that so much of it had gone on supporting her brother. She had managed to buy Tommy a ground-floor flat with adaptations made to cater for his lack of mobility. He had tried to tell her not to but she had insisted. He needed looking after. He always had, even from a young child. He had never had her strength of character, and after his accident Grace had been all too willing to carry on caretaking duties.

After all, who else was going to look after him? And with her mother on the other side of the world, Tommy was the only family she had left here.

So not only had she sacrificed her own dream of owning a property to help him out and buy him somewhere to live, but then there had been the bills for the private therapist, which hadn't come cheap.

Fortunately, those had decreased from twice a week to once a week, but there was no way they could be halted for good. How else would her brother ever be in the right frame of mind to deal with the setbacks he had suffered? To fully pick himself up and look to a future very different from the one he had planned?

'I would rather not on the phone, no.' Then the briefest of pauses. 'Am I interrupting something?'

'I was just about to start preparing my dinner,' she said on a sigh.

'In which case, I have an idea. Why don't you meet me at the office in an hour and I'll make sure to get some food in? I know how inconvenient this is and you have my apologies but, like I've said, I wouldn't have called if it wasn't necessary.'

'I suppose…if it's urgent…'

'Great. See you there in an hour. French, Indian or Italian?'

'Sorry?'

'Choice of food. French, Indian or Italian?'

'I honestly am not fussy.'

'One of your many endearing traits and probably why we work so well together. Leave it to me. I'll make sure neither of us goes hungry.'

At which point he cut the call and, for a few seconds, Grace stared at the phone in her hand before leaping to her feet to hurriedly tidy the kitchen and then get changed into something…

Into what?

Her usual outfit? Knee-length skirt and tidy blouse and *I-mean-business* flat black pumps?

On a Friday evening?

Reluctantly Grace chose jeans and a slim-fitting tee shirt and an old tan bomber jacket she had inherited from her mother, just in case it was cold by the time she left.

For once, she had no idea what she was letting herself in for. Nico, for all his colourful love life and ever-changing parade of beauties, was utterly predictable when it came to his working life.

Nothing ever came in the way of it. The women he dated were confined to life outside his cutting-edge offices and on the rare occasions when one of them had ventured where angels feared to tread, she had learnt that such errors of judgement were not to be repeated.

So what was this about? How could it be *yes and no* when it came to work? He wasn't a *yes and no* man.

It felt strange to be hurrying to the office, dressed down, without her stern work clothes in place, as secure and as reassuring as a chastity belt, keeping her imagination in check and reminding her of the differences between them.

Over the past few weeks, the lines between them had taken a knocking and while she knew that Nico was oblivious to those subtle changes, it wasn't so for her.

She noticed every time the conversation between them veered even slightly off-piste. He had asked her, in passing, whether she had been out with anyone else and how could she refuse to answer when that door had been opened?

If she had thought that being more open might have ushered in a more normal state of affairs for her, then she had been mistaken, because closing some of the distance had only made her all the more conscious of her attraction to him and of the pointlessness of it.

What he saw as normal office banter, she saw as a threat to her composure. When he perched on the edge of the desk and asked her casually about her weekend, all she could feel was the racing of her pulse as she tried to ward off the suffocating effect his proximity had on her.

So right now, jeans and a tee shirt and a bomber jacket felt all wrong as she pushed open the glass doors to the building, flashing her official card to the security guard, who knew her anyway and just smiled and waved her through.

Nico was waiting when, exactly an hour after he had called her, she pushed open the door to the office.

He had never seen her here, in these surroundings, in anything other than a suit of some kind so he did a double take at the jeans and tee shirt and the old leather jacket slung over her shoulder.

In fact, for a few seconds, he was lost for words. First a flowered dress with strappy sleeves and now faded jeans and a bomber jacket…?

How much more wrong could he have been about

her? More to the point, how much more egotistic could he have been in vaguely thinking that when she wasn't within the confines of these office walls, she somehow remained prim, prissy and mysteriously clad in skirts and blouses?

'Good timing.' He stood up and flexed his muscles, easing away some of the tension that had been building ever since the call from his father. 'The food has just arrived. We can eat and…talk.'

He strolled towards the floor-to-ceiling window and remained there for a few seconds, watching as she ditched the bomber jacket, admiring the ballet-like gracefulness of her movements, so much more noticeable in what she was wearing. The faded jeans fitted her like a second skin, emphasising the length and slimness of her legs, and the tee shirt clung invitingly to breasts that were just about a handful.

He had to tear his eyes away, tell himself to focus.

He nodded towards the sitting area that adjoined the office, where the food was still in neat black and gold containers, bearing the crest of one of the go-to restaurants he used when he wanted food brought in for him.

She preceded him through to the little table and hovered, waiting for him to take the lead and no nearer to figuring out what exactly was going on.

'Italian,' Nico said, settling into the chair facing hers, separated by the squat, rectangular glass-and-chrome table between them.

He flipped open the lids of the containers and nodded to her to help herself.

'There was no need for anything fancy, Nico, or anything at all.'

'Least I could do for dragging you out of your house.'

'You still have to tell me what this is all about.'

For once, Nico's natural assertiveness abandoned him and Grace saw a shadow of hesitation. Her curiosity was piqued. Hesitant was the very last thing her boss ever was. A charging rhino displayed more hesitancy than Nico Doukas.

For a few seconds he didn't answer, just took his time dishing out food and then strolling to the concealed fridge where he kept several bottles of wine for clients. He lifted one and she shook her head.

'I'll never be able to concentrate if I have a glass of wine,' she said politely.

'In which case, you'll have to excuse me if I don't follow suit,' he returned wryly as he poured himself a glass and handed her some water. 'I got a call from my father today.' There was a dark flush etched across his sharp cheekbones and Grace stilled and looked at him with a slight frown.

'Is everything all right? Is it your mother?' she asked quietly, already braced for bad news. He had gone to Greece previously to visit them and she knew that his mother had recently had a bout of ill health. Nico rarely touched on the subject of his parents, but she had seen from the look in his eyes when he had told her of the reason for his week away from the desk that he cared deeply about them. When he had returned, it had been business as normal. Her enquiries about how things were with them both had been met with a polite but unembroidered response and she had got the message that that was an area that he wished to keep to himself.

He put so much out there in the public domain and yet so much was carefully concealed.

'My mother is doing well. Improving by the day but still in need of rest after her operation. No, this is about my uncle.'

'You have *an uncle*?'

'It's not that unusual,' Nico said wryly, 'although the use of the present tense doesn't apply in this instance. My uncle died two days ago and, with my mother still recovering, it's fallen upon me to wrap up his affairs.'

'Nico, I don't understand. I'm, of course, very sorry for your loss, but I'm not sure why I had to rush over here on a Friday evening so that you could tell me this.' Grace was genuinely confused, yet there was a thread of pleasure underlying her bewilderment.

Had she been the first person he'd chosen to call to share this heartbreaking news with?

She remembered how he had rushed to save her from herself and from Victor when he'd correctly clocked that she'd been in an uncomfortable situation. It had been an intuitive reaction. He had even dispatched his own date so that he could mount the stallion and charge to her rescue!

Did he actually care about her on some level that he wasn't conscious of?

It was completely taboo to be thinking like this, but Grace couldn't stop a shiver of forbidden pleasure from racing through her, like a dangerously addictive drug.

Belatedly she remembered Cecily and the eternal search for Mr Right. There had been so many times when optimism had trumped reality. Too many to count. Grace had always had to pick up the pieces when the bubble had burst and her mother had finally accepted that the guy who'd paid her tons of compliments and taken her out for two meals wasn't going to be putting a ring on her finger. It had taken her even longer to realise that she was better off without that particular Mr Right. It had always been a long, slow process and watching hope die had taught Grace a thousand and one life lessons.

Never, in all the time she had harboured her secret crush, had she felt herself in jeopardy.

How could you be in any danger of *anything* when you were having secret fantasies about some guy who never spared you a second glance?

Except when asking whether you'd checked the company accounts for his most recent takeover. Or sorted those supply chains that were screwed up because of a boat being docked too long somewhere too far away because of bad weather.

So she'd woken up and realised that the secret fantasies had had their day and the time had come to try and find the real thing, a real, living, breathing guy with whom she could have a complete relationship. She'd accepted that Nico had been a useful, innocent distraction at a time when her life had been in turmoil.

But everything had been turned on its head and nothing was what it had been before. He had crashed through all the red tape and *Keep Out* signs and now...

Her awareness was so close to the surface. She could sense the shift between them even though she'd done her best to return to where they had been before. When he came close to her, she could feel a thread of electric charge pushing between them, a low vibration that meant she was on red-hot alert every single second of every single day she was in his company.

This was no longer an innocent distraction.

Now her harmless crush felt dangerous.

Now, for the first time, Grace felt as though she was being called upon to test all those life lessons she thought she had learnt from her mother's adventures.

She reined in her thoughts and returned to the matter at hand. 'And why can't your dad handle the situation? I know your mother's recovering but surely the funeral arrangements can largely be done over the phone? From what I've seen of your mother when she's been over here, I don't think she's going to go to pieces if she's left on her own for a couple of hours. Do you? When they were over before I remember her telling him that there was no need for him to follow her everywhere…and how could he possibly be interested in what was happening in ladies' fashionwear at Selfridges.'

Nico smiled, momentarily diverted as he thought about the dynamics between his parents.

If his uncle had gone off the rails, his father had done completely the opposite.

It had taken the joker in the pack to produce the King of Spades, needed to assume control and get things on track.

Maybe his father would have been the man he had become whatever the circumstances, but maybe Sander had done that. There had been a vacancy for someone strong to take the reins and his father had stepped up to the plate because, frankly, he hadn't had much choice.

He had chosen his wife with his head. He had put his emotions to one side and opted for a woman from the same elevated, wealthy background who knew the ropes. No room for demanding hysterics, just calm support where it was needed. He couldn't remember a single instance of his parents rowing. When his father had worked late, his mother had patiently been there, her role to take the pressure off and not pile it on by demanding he focus on *her*.

From his own experience, Nico could appreciate how important it was to marry a suitable woman.

You could have affairs with women who wanted to be the centre of attention, but those were affairs.

If he had ever thought that his father's life might have been too regimented, his own fling all those years ago, when he had been prepared to give love and emotions a go, had taught him otherwise. Eva had wanted all of him. She had demanded proof of his devotion and insisted that work be delegated to the back burner. She was either everything to him or nothing at all. But at the helm of his own burgeoning business, which had demanded many long nights and gruelling commitments, Nico had come to realise that he was just too imbued with a sense of responsibility to ditch everything because a woman needed him to prove himself.

Now he accepted that he was a workaholic and, as such, when he decided to move from having flings to settling down, it would be with a woman who had no illusions about what she was letting herself in for.

A lifetime of having everything money could buy. In return, he would get a dependable woman who would accept his priorities and live with them.

His parents loved one another. It had been a good relationship and a wise choice because crazy emotions hadn't been in charge, just common sense and goodwill on both sides.

From that had sprung just the sort of marital stability that worked.

'I forgot about that. Of course, in normal circumstances my father could deal with all of this. Unfortunately, things are a little different in this case and I've asked you here urgently because this involves you. I will have to carry on working while I'm dealing with Sander's situation, and I'll need you there in a working capacity. I can't afford to go off radar for a week. Aside from which, there will be certain business matters to handle when we get there. Not extensive but there'll be business to be done and you know how my work suffers when you're not around. I need you by my side or I become a nervous wreck and end up comfort eating.' He shot her a disarming grin.

Of course, this boiled down to work, Grace thought bracingly. What else? Had she really believed that Nico had suddenly called her up because he'd wanted someone to talk to? To share with?

'There? Where's *there*?'

'The Bahamas,' he said, sitting back in the chair, having finished everything on his plate. 'And the reason this couldn't wait is because time is of the essence. I hope your passport is in date because you'll need to book me on the first flight to Nassau tomorrow and you can follow on Monday. I realise this might come as a bolt from the blue but… any questions?'

CHAPTER FOUR

ANY QUESTIONS?

Two and a half days later, Grace wondered how it was that with so many questions, she had managed to ask precious few.

Caught on the back foot, she had gaped at him in astounded silence while he had filled the yawning space with a detailed explanation of why, exactly, he needed her there.

The deals that were coming to fruition, the due diligence needed on several takeovers, and she had to be at ground zero to handle the paperwork because the damned lawyers were prone to chopping and changing...not to mention the running of the family business, with difficulties cropping up because of supply-chain issues. And then there would be some business stuff of his uncle's to sort out. Nothing much, but it would still have to be done. He couldn't do any of that without her, he had concluded in a voice that had left her in no doubt that a negative response would not be countenanced.

She had thought of Tommy and demanded to know just how long the trip would last.

'Why?' Nico had queried, eyebrows raised. 'Have you got unavoidable plans if it takes five days instead of four?'

'Are you saying we'll be away for four days?'

'I'm saying,' he had responded in an inflexible voice, the voice of the boss who paid the bills, 'that we'll be away for just as long as it takes to conclude this business. My father would have gone himself but he is in no place to leave my mother convalescing on her own. The burden falls to me, and you'll be coming because you work for me and I need to carry on working over there.'

Nico had never mentioned an uncle. Why would he? Grace supposed. It was none of her business. But what was his uncle doing out in the Bahamas? Why wasn't he part of the family business either in Greece or here in London?

Nico hadn't volunteered an explanation but he had softened enough to ask, 'Why are you concerned about the length of time we'll be gone? I can guarantee that it won't be longer than five days. I have no desire to be out of London for any longer. If I'm honest, I could do without this intrusion into my working schedule, but needs must.'

He'd shrugged and when his dark eyes had rested on her face she'd seen him thinking, *Why so concerned about how long this will take?*

'Has another Mr Internet stepped into the pic-

ture?' he'd asked silkily and Grace had glared at him,
which had given him his answer without him having
to ask further. She realised how effective that had
been on shutting the conversation down and making
sure she didn't ask any more questions.

The following day, she had duly booked the
flights and he had texted to tell her that there was
no need for a hotel. Flights sorted, he would deal
with the rest of the details. She should just get her
things together and he would ensure all the necessary
protocol to get her to him on the Monday evening.

So here she was now, after an uneventful and
comfortable trip to Nassau.

The seat-belt sign was going on and the captain
was interrupting the film she had been watching to
tell them how close they were to landing and what
the weather was doing and what the local time was.

It had been a long time since Grace had been on
a plane. A long time since she had had any real holiday to speak of. Ibiza with three friends five years
ago felt like a lifetime away. Since then, her money
had been directed at all the costly expenditure asso-
ciated with looking after her brother, the buying of
the house, the tailoring of the space to suit his needs
and of course the private therapy sessions. None of it
came cheap and while her own life had largely been
on hold, the prospect of going anywhere abroad on
a holiday had been vanishingly slim.

Ever since Nico had left her in the office, leaving behind him a state of low-level panic at this de-

parture from her prized comfort zone, she had been busy fretting. Fretting about the fact that she would be with him in such different surroundings. Fretting about how that was going to feel. Fretting about the clothes to be packed, about an itinerary she couldn't quite manage to work out. There would be no comforting office environment in which to feel safe. The barriers between them had already taken a bit of a knock and this drastic change to the normal routine made her feel uneasy and apprehensive.

Now, though, as she snapped shut the seat belt and gazed down out of the window, she was infused with a bubble of excitement.

The plane dipped and she was offered a view of lush green set against a backdrop of startling aquamarine. Trees and mountains rising from an ocean of tranquil turquoise and, even from dizzying heights, the water was such a dazzling blue that it took her breath away.

Nico had told her that her only responsibility was to book the flight for them both.

She'd assumed that he had contacts on the island. If his uncle had lived there, for whatever reason, then he would probably know people, people who would be able to arrange accommodation for them far more satisfactorily than she could.

As the plane rolled to a stop, slowly positioning itself in front of the airport terminal, she wondered what this accommodation was going to look like.

Who was going to meet her at the airport? Would

Nico be there? The thought of him made her heart beat a little faster.

The heat struck her with force as she stepped out of the plane. This wasn't the polite summer sun she had left behind in London. This was tropical heat, still and fierce and smelling different somehow. She breathed in and that bubble of excitement swelled a little bit more and she had to sternly remind herself that this wasn't a holiday. This was about work.

She was wearing a pair of light cotton trousers and a loose linen shirt. Within seconds of being in the blasting heat, a couple of minutes out in the open between the plane and the airport, she could feel herself perspiring. It was joyful to be inside the cold terminal. Not knowing quite what to expect, she was surprised when she was ushered through a fast lane to exit immigration and security in re-cord time. She'd brought one bag into which she had crammed her usual summer wardrobe of light suits along with a couple of summery dresses and some sandals. Work-ready gear for a tropical island. She was already beginning to suspect that her choices might not have been the most sensible, given the weather.

There was no Nico waiting for her but instead a young, smiling man in a uniform of Bermuda shorts and an open-necked shirt who leapt towards her, flashing identification and a personal letter from Nico explaining that he couldn't make it to the air-port, but giving her details of her onward journey.

It was all a blur. Grace was tired yet energised at the same time. Outside the airport, the noises and the sounds and the sights were all so unfamiliar that she could have been on another planet. Everything was in Technicolour, the shimmering tarmac of the road against the brightest of lush green of trees and bushes and weeds and flowers growing in abundance wherever a spot of earth could hold a root. Cars came and went, as did people, coming and leaving, pulling bags and hugging and saying goodbye, a riot of activity against a backdrop of tropical splendour.

She gaped. Where were they going? Where would she be staying?

Not here, not on the main island. She discovered that soon enough because as they walked Curtis told her that he would be taking her to a private airfield, where she would get an island hopper that would take her to one of the smaller islands.

'Mr Nico's there, waiting for you. He tells me you can stay the night in Nassau, fly tomorrow. You want to do that?'

But Grace was eager to finish the trip without interruption and that seemed to have been the message conveyed to Curtis from Nico because there was an acceptance that she would accompany him, which she did.

All her senses were accosted by the shimmering beauty of her surroundings. She could smell the salty sea in the air and she didn't know where to look as she followed Curtis to another part of the airfield, towards a small bank of island hoppers.

'Where are we going?' she asked breathlessly as she followed him to one of the tiny planes, where a pilot was waiting to take off.

'Another of the islands.' He flashed her a broad, proud smile. 'Plenty islands here. Very beautiful. Mr Nico waiting for you on one of them. You going to be very happy when you get there, Miss Grace.'

Grace smiled back and wondered if she should tell him that she was there for work reasons, but chose not to, and follow-up conversation was lost, anyway, in the hustle and bustle of leaving the airport.

It was a brief flight, bumpy as the little plane barely skimmed the top of the clouds, and from her vantage point she could gaze down at an expanse of aquamarine ocean, so clear that she could discern the shapes of rocks and reefs under the surface. The occasional boat dotted the surface, the interruption of islands like pearls strung into a necklace surrounded by water.

That excitement again, reminding her of just how much she had sacrificed over the years.

It had been a gradual build-up. She had had her childhood snatched from her simply because Cecily had been an irresponsible parent. Her mother had cornered the market on having fun, and in the process had deprived her of her own chances to have it. From latchkey kid, she had assumed responsibilities way beyond the pale from far too young an age, and just when she could have really begun to enjoy her life, to live it free from having to be the resident caretaker, her brother had had his accident and, shortly after, her mother had left the country.

And in her gaily departed wake, amidst the flurry of hugs and kisses and dabbed tears, Grace had quietly resigned herself to the door being shut on her dreams of breaking free.

Someone would have to look out for Tommy and her mother wasn't going to suddenly start auditioning for the Mother of the Year award when she'd spent her entire life turning down the role.

So this—however apprehensive she felt about the change to her routine—felt like a holiday and made her heart soar.

Too soon the little plane was dipping down and the pilot was telling her to make sure she was fastened in.

'These runways are small.' He turned to grin at her. 'Sometimes you have to screech to a stop before you hit sea.'

'That's comforting.' Grace laughed but he wasn't kidding and the shriek of brakes as the aircraft shuddered to a stop made her clutch the arms of her seat and squeeze shut her eyes.

She opened them to see Nico.

He was walking towards the plane and she wondered whether it was her imagination or whether a couple of days in the sun had turned him an even deeper shade of bronze.

He looked impossibly sexy. His black, too long hair had curled a little in the heat and he was wearing a pair of dark sunglasses, which made it impossible for her to see his eyes. He was in the outfit of nearly everyone else she'd seen—slim, tailored pale shorts and a tee shirt—and as he stopped by the plane, he shoved the shades up and squinted into the sun towards her.

Grace pulled back from the window. The pilot was already opening the door and a burst of hot air flooded in as she quickly scrambled to her feet, reaching for her bag and holding it as close to her as a talisman as she carefully dipped out of the plane and gingerly walked down the metal steps.

On the last step, Nico reached out for her hand, a polite gesture that still sent a shock wave of heat through her.

'Here in one piece, I see,' he murmured, sunglasses back in place, which made her feel immediately disadvantaged.

'The arrangements went very smoothly.' Grace looked away and ran her finger under the collar of her shirt, aiming for some much-needed ventilation.

Looking at her, Nico had to stop himself from bursting into laughter. Honestly. What on earth was she wearing? Surely she would have twigged that a tropical island was no place for starchy work clothes in which she would be reduced to a puddle of sweat the very second she was exposed to the fierce heat? He shoved his hands into the pockets of his shorts and politely made some chit-chat about flying and aeroplane meals as they headed towards the small SUV parked at an angle in the distance.

Nevertheless, he couldn't resist saying, as they approached the car, 'You must be hot.' He slid his eyes across to her and saw the delicate blush. 'I'm very much hoping,' he murmured gravely, 'that this isn't going to be your standard dress code.'

'I'm not at all hot,' Grace lied.

'We're not going to be in the formal setting of an office,' Nico continued, noting the way she blew the hair from her face and continued fiddling with the collar of her prissy shirt, 'so you're allowed to wear more informal clothing.'

'I thought we were going to be working while we were here.'

'We are, but not in the conventional setting of an office. Of course, the hotel has somewhere we can work but...' Nico paused, opened the door of the four-wheel drive, flung her case in the back seat and sauntered round to the driver's side. He turned to her before starting the engine, his hand loose on the steering wheel. 'But the hotel isn't quite what I had imagined.'

He turned on the engine and accelerated out of the airfield. No air conditioning. The windows were open and as the car bumped up speed Grace's hair was blown back by the warm air.

'What do you mean?'

'I mean…' Nico shrugged, eyes on the road as he manoeuvred the car away from the airport and along the steaming tarmac framed with lush green, beyond which was the flat blue sea '… I was expecting something slightly…bigger and more…how shall I put it? More…tourist-oriented than what confronted me.'

'But how could you not know what to expect? Haven't you been here before?'

Nico took his time answering. When he was growing up, mention of his black sheep uncle had always been accompanied by disapproving frowns and muttered oaths. He knew the story of Sander as much as everyone else did. A waste of space whose vices had come close to threatening the survival of the family empire. A man so addicted to self-indulgence and so willing to fight tooth and nail to feed his habits that extreme measures had been taken to limit the damage he could do. To get rid of him.

Raised on a diet of self-discipline and the mantra that doing the right thing involved making sure the company was never jeopardised because it was bigger than just the Doukas family, Nico found everything his uncle had represented personally unacceptable.

Yes, Nico enjoyed a playboy lifestyle. Yes, he enjoyed women and he enjoyed sex, but when it came to the family holdings and his own considerable empire he had always known that his duty lay in sober considerations. There would be no room for anything other than the path his own father had followed. He would wed a suitable wife and emotions would never be allowed to destroy what had been built.

Secretly, Nico had a deeply buried fear that his own personality was far more like his uncle's than he cared to admit, which made it all the more imperative that he maintain self-control.

He slanted assessing eyes at his companion in the passenger seat because she had asked a valid question.

It was ironic that, while she knew so much about the way he worked and, frankly, the person he was, she knew so little about the actual nuts and bolts of his life. Although, as she had rightly pointed out, he kept to himself exactly what he didn't want the rest of the world to know. When he thought about it, she was different from any of the other women who had entered and departed his life. Actually, she was *very* different, because she actually knew him, with the kind of intangible familiarity that came when you worked alongside someone for a long time. She could practically read his mind when it came to certain things!

But when it came to the details of his personal life? Those were closely guarded. Nico had long ago worked out that to maintain control of your life where it mattered, it was important that you let nothing go. Start opening up and things stood a good chance of unravelling like a ball of wool.

However, here they were and his secretary, until recently a closed book, would inevitably end up knowing something of his life whether he felt inclined to impart the information or not.

Nico told himself that it didn't matter. Grace was his secretary. She wasn't his lover. Lovers clung to confidences, read meaning into them, hoped for more. As his secretary, she would listen, skim over the personal and focus on the practical, namely the business of sorting out the hotel along with everything else.

Except things had changed between them...hadn't they?

Nico shrugged off that fleeting thought.

They were driving slowly, the winding road fringed with trees and foliage, swaying palms tilting up to the blue sky, houses interrupting the green landscape.

He'd only been on the island for a day and a half, but he already knew how to get around it because it was small and the main road was the artery from which smaller roads meandered off into the hills.

He took one of those side roads now.

At the corner, in front of a patchwork of flimsy houses, a dark-skinned woman was sitting in front of a stall that was bursting with vibrant colours of fresh fruit and vegetables.

Ahead, the broad, smooth road turned into a more winding track, although it was still possible for two cars to pass one another. Not that the island was bustling with traffic. The small town was busy, with a humming central market, but away from that the tributary of roads, winding through little pockets of houses and shops and all leading to beaches of some sort, were largely quiet.

'I've never been to this part of the world before,' Nico admitted heavily. 'Why would I?'

'But surely if your uncle lived here... I mean, it's so beautiful...' She slid a sidelong glance at him and smiled. 'If I had a close relative living in a place like this, you'd have to lock me up and throw away the key to stop me from flying over and demanding ac-commodation at least once a year.'

Nico burst out laughing. 'I can't relax where there's nothing to do,' he admitted. 'Lying on a beach staring at the sea isn't my thing.'

'I can't think of anything better,' Grace mused. She shrugged. 'But I guess to each their own. Why have you never been here? Aside from not liking holidays that aren't action-packed? Didn't you want to visit your uncle? Or did he prefer to go to Greece to see your family? What brought him over here in the first place?'

'Long story.'

'And one you don't want to tell? Nico, it doesn't matter.'

Nico glanced across to her, but she was turned away, her head slightly tilted to appreciate the warm breeze against her face, her eyes half closed as she gazed out at the stupendous passing scenery.

She hadn't pushed for details and suddenly he felt an urge to do more than just volunteer scant information because, really, what business was his background story to her?

For once, slamming the door on a question that breached his boundary lines felt like overkill.

Besides, did she care one way or another if he answered? Then he thought of that simmering spark that had been lit under them weeks before, the spark she'd made sure to douse.

Maybe she did care...maybe more than those cool eyes revealed...

There was a soft smile tugging her lips as she enjoyed the heat and the sprawling, lush beauty.

He swerved off the road, bumped the four-wheel drive to a stop on the grassy verge.

'What are you doing?' Grace's head snapped round and she stared at him in some consternation.

'Two things. First...' He reached past her to open her door and felt the slight brush of her body against his arm. He impatiently dismissed the sharp physical awareness that accompanied this involuntary touch. 'First...this is a good lookout point to see something of the island from above.' He nodded to a bench that was tilted at a precarious angle a little further down the verge. He slung his long, muscular body out of the Jeep but then promptly turned so that he was looking at her, one arm resting casually on the open door as he leant down towards her. 'I found this spot accidentally when I stopped off to take a call. Come have a look. You'll be impressed. I guarantee that.'

* * *

Grace obligingly stepped out of the car. Despite the refreshing breeze, fragrant with the scent of the colourful flowers by the roadside, the heat was still a solid wall that burnt through the trousers and the too thick blouse. She fanned herself and walked to the bench, which was perfectly solid once she gingerly perched on it, despite outward appearances.

'It's so quiet here. It's like life slowed right down,' she murmured, dutifully looking down and drawing breath at the spectacular scenery. She had been acutely conscious of Nico perching next to her on the bench, the heat radiating from his body, the muscular brown thighs so close to her, the way dark hair curled around the dull matt of his watch strap.

Not now. As she stared down, all she could see was the splendid turquoise of ocean, glittering in the distance, bright blue against dark green…the sway of upright palm trees and the little roads intersecting the landscape like veins and arteries, bordered with small houses, some brightly painted, some white-washed.

'Small island with not that many inhabitants. The tourist trade is booming because there are a lot of people who want this sort of final escape but, even with that, it's still a very peaceful place. Must have to do with the arduous business of actually getting here. Plane and then another plane or a boat across. A lot of people prefer the one-stop destination.'

Grace glanced across at him and shivered at the aquiline perfection of his profile.

Her eyes drifted to his legs, stretched out in front, so brown with a sprinkling of dark hair that made her imagination take flight as she pictured what the rest of his body might look like. She quickly looked away and fanned herself in a desultory attempt to cool down.

'What was the second thing you wanted to say to me?'

She felt his eyes on her as he shifted, turning to face her, his hands clasped behind his head.

The tee shirt rode up and she glimpsed a slither of flat, hard belly.

'You asked me why I've never been here. You're curious and I don't blame you. I've never been here because my uncle was banished here,' Nico said quietly. 'Exiled from doing damage to the family company because of his bad habits.'

Grace inhaled sharply and turned to look at him. Their eyes collided but she didn't look away. This was absolutely the first time Nico had ever volunteered anything remotely revealing about himself. The ground seemed to shift a little under her feet.

'What do you mean?' She kept her voice neutral even though curiosity was running riot inside her.

'Sander was a weak man,' Nico said flatly. 'No self-control. He enjoyed drink, drugs and women and he allowed his enjoyment to take over his life, to kill all sense of responsibility. He couldn't give a damn whose lives got destroyed because he was too busy squandering his share of the company that had been left to him when my grandfather died.' When Nico looked at her, his dark eyes brooding, unforgiving, it was to find her gazing straight back at him, her interest calm and modulated, encouraging without giving him the impression that she was desperate to hear more.

'Were it not for my father, God knows he would have ended up dragging the company into the dirt. If it was just a question of Sander on a path to his own self destruction, then the solution might have been less dramatic, but the fact is that my uncle's self-destruction would have involved more than just himself.'

'So your father…?'

'Annexed him, having spent years picking up the pieces. Made it worse that Sander was the older by five years. Of course, he had more than enough money to do whatever he wanted, but the flow of money was controlled. The rift caused was papered over in time but, as brothers, the connection had been broken for ever. I'm not sure whether my parents ever came over here at all. Possibly they communicated by email. I don't know.'

'How old were you when all of this happened?'

'Very young.'

'How sad.' Grace meant it. She thought of her own brother and the loyalty that was so deeply rooted inside her that there was no way she could ever *annex* him. It very much sounded as though Nico was fashioned in the same mould as his father, ruthless when it came to protecting the interests of the family company.

For a split second Grace was tempted to confide, and she pulled herself back from the brink before reckless impulse could take over.

Nico might be sharing this with her now, but it was because they were here and the backstory was tied up to a bigger picture.

Would he welcome a sudden sharing of confidences? Would he expect his cool, calm secretary to start pouring her heart out? No. He'd be appalled.

'There's no room for superfluous emotion when other people's lives are involved.' He paused and said, with a hitch in his usually composed voice, 'My father told me that one of the guys who worked for my uncle lost everything because Sander had dissolved that branch of the organisation for no other reason than to fund a gambling debt. The guy committed suicide.'

'My goodness!'

'Lessons learnt when it comes to the weakness of allowing emotion to run your life,' Nico told her darkly. 'My father made sensible choices. Necessary sacrifices.' He shrugged and half smiled as though slightly embarrassed by confidences he was unaccustomed to sharing. 'At any rate, this all happened a long time ago. Sander has been here doing his own thing and this is the first time I've had any real idea of how he's spent the years since he disappeared from Greece.'

Grace didn't say anything. She thought that tangled in that simple statement, woven into what Nico had just told her, one thing emerged very clearly.

Not only did Nico not know his uncle, but neither did he respect him. His uncle had been ruled by excess and that, for Nico, was abhorrent.

Was that why, underneath the easy charm, there was a core of icy steel that made him so inaccessible? Had it been drummed into him from an early age that self-control was the only thing that mattered?

Grace wondered whether it was that very self-control that made it possible for Nico to have his flings without danger of involvement.

Did he ambush his own chances at having a lasting relationship by dating women he knew would always be temporary visitors in his life? While he bided his time for the woman he would eventually marry? A woman who would be happy to take second place to his work and forgive him his inability to form any close bond? Grace mentally wished this poor, hypothetical woman good luck with choosing a life like that.

She might have developed an inconvenient crush on her handsome and charismatic boss, but there was no way she could ever be in danger of harbouring any deeper, darker feelings for him because she was smart enough to realise that a guy like him, in

the end, was the antithesis of everything she looked
for in a for-ever guy.

She averted her eyes and returned her gaze to the
splendid vista in front of her. 'But weren't you curious to find out what happened to him?'

'He was sidelined and that was sufficient. Get too
bogged down in detail and chances are you never
surface. That said, I assumed Sander was involved
in a more comprehensive business than it turns out.'
Nico glanced at her and grinned. 'No idea why, to be
honest. Possibly because over the years he suppos-
edly straightened himself out and the hotel, from all
accounts, was actually making a decent profit. Now
I'm here, I've discovered that the hotel is rather more
of an…ah…upmarket boarding house and the money
lies in the bar adjoining it and a fishing boat business, which has held its own over the years.'

'What is your role in…um…this? Are you going
to dispose of the business?'

'What else?' Nico shrugged. 'It's of no use to me
and I certainly don't envisage my father wanting anything to do with it. At any rate, that's where we'll be
staying so I hope you're not expecting much by way
of luxury because if you are, then you're going to be
mightily disappointed.'

Grace returned his stare with sudden amusement.
'Now who's misreading who?' She half smiled. 'Do
you really see me as a snob? I don't care where we
stay. We're here to do a job and, as you've assured
me, we won't be here for longer than a handful of

days. I think I'm more than capable of staying in an upmarket boarding house for the duration.' She stood up and stretched and then waited a few seconds before Nico followed suit. 'When we get there, what's the plan? I'm very happy to shower, change and begin work immediately.'

'I'm sure you are,' Nico murmured with just the slightest hint of laughter in his voice. 'You're certainly dressed for it but no. I think we can start work tomorrow. For the rest of the day? You could always try and relax…'

CHAPTER FIVE

IT BECAME VERY clear over the next twenty-four hours just how dismissive Nico was of the uncle he had never known.

Naturally, in the process of winding up the hotel and the various business concerns Sander had built over the years, he had had to consult with various members of staff. Any mention of his uncle from any employee was met with polite, stony silence unless it pertained to business. Fond reminiscing was shut down at source. Grace wondered whether Nico was even capable of seeing that or whether his inherited disdain for Sander Doukas ran so deep that he wasn't aware of his prejudices.

He would begin the process of finding a buyer for the various concerns, he had assured Steve Donnelly, the smiling, affable manager of the hotel who also seemed to fill a number of varied roles, including captain of the small six-boat fishing rental and head of the hotel kitchen. No one would lose their jobs if he could help it but, of course, that wasn't going to be in his remit. He could only do so much.

Grace thought that if things continued going at the speed they were currently going, then everything would be wrapped up in a couple of days because the nuts and bolts of whatever deals were agreed with potential buyers would be handled by lawyers, who were already on standby.

. And several of those potential buyers, Nico had briefed her only an hour ago, had already been found.

Now, sitting here on the wooden veranda of the hotel, waiting for Nico, who was going to be her dinner companion on her first real night here, she remembered her excitement when the plane had begun to descend to Nassau, with a little twinge of sadness. .

Her only view of the sea had been in passing, as she had strolled out of the hotel at midday to breathe in the sun and the salt and the heady scent of the tropical blooms that surrounded the hotel.

In the distance a marching army of upright coconut trees was starkly silhouetted against the deep purple, indigo and navy blue of a twilit sky.

The 'upmarket boarding house' could not have been lovelier, as far as Grace was concerned. Nico might favour the impersonal opulence of a five-star modern hotel with its cold marble, glass and granite, but, for her, this place was wonderful. It was small, with maybe a dozen rooms at the most, all tiny suites, some of them self-contained and positioned in between coconut trees, others within the main body of the hotel. Each was quirky and different, but all were tropical in flavour, with bamboo and rattan furnishings and paintings by local artists.

There were mosquito nets around the four-poster beds and overhead fans instead of air conditioning and always the sound of the sea, which was accessible on foot, just a ten-minute walk away.

Not that Grace had had the chance to explore yet.

Probably wouldn't because it was obvious that Nico couldn't wait to clear off as fast as possible.

The veranda was broad, big enough for clusters of chairs and sofas and little tables. With the business on the brink of being sold, the only visitors were the ones currently wrapping up their stay, so the hotel was only half full.

Bookings had been halted.

Right now, there were a few people further along the veranda, sipping cocktails and chatting in low voices.

Grace was barely aware of them. She was so captivated by the lazy stirring of the coconut trees and the quiet insistent hush of waves gently breaking, ebbing and flowing, that Nico's voice made her jump and she spun round to see him standing behind her.

He was nursing a drink and in a pair of light-coloured trousers and a black collared polo shirt.

He looked effortlessly and unfairly impressive as he stared down at her, his face unreadable because the light from the hotel was behind him.

* * *

'You're still in work clothes.'

She'd certainly come prepared to work because the travelling attire had been replaced, today, by a similar uniform of linen trousers and a blouse neatly tucked into the waistband. Buttons firmly done up to the neck.

And here she was now, in yet another pair of trousers and another blouse.

The colour was less regimental but the flavour was still *let's-stick-to-business*.

He grinned, sipped his whisky and sauntered to pull up a chair, sitting down alongside her.

'I'm beginning to feel a little guilty that I haven't packed any of my suits.'

'Ha ha, that's hilarious. These aren't work clothes, Nico.'

'My mistake. At close range, it's hard to see much difference. It's been a long day.' He was still grinning as he signalled to a passing waiter for the drinks menu. 'Time to relax. What do you want to drink?'

'I'll have a…tropical fruit punch,' Grace said.

'With lashings of rum,' Nico tacked on, eyebrows raised with amusement as she predictably began to huff. 'You can't sit here, with the sun settling on the horizon and a balmy breeze blowing, and order a glass of juice.'

'I…'

'Yes, you're here to work, but you're not working now and you deserve to let go after the long day we've had, so I won't hear of you having some squash instead of something long and cold and relaxing. Live a little, Grace.' His eyebrows shot up with barely contained amusement. He wondered which of his outrageous encouragements would get under her skin more and he had no idea why he was so tempted to flirt with her wrath now but watching her all day…had been strangely intoxicating. Something about the way she moved, the oddly prissy clothes, her habit of absently puffing her hair from her forehead and tucking it behind her ears when she was concentrating…

True to form, she had immersed herself in work and true to form they had worked quietly and efficiently together, building up the blocks for selling the various companies, liaising with local lawyers virtually and arranging meetings for the following day as everything sped ahead, promising an early conclusion to business here.

In the blink of an eye they'd be back in London. She'd be sitting dutifully in front of his desk, going through emails and noting what had to be done on what deal or other he was working on, and gradually that small window through which he had glimpsed something of the *real* Grace Brown would be closed for ever.

'And back to the work clothes that aren't work clothes. Look around you. Bold colours…shorts… flip-flops… It's not the sort of place that screams conference-table dress code.'

* * *

Grace felt the sting of embarrassment and hurt prick her eyelids.

She looked away briefly and started when she felt Nico's hand on hers. This time when their eyes met, the lazy, amused smile had left his lips.

'I'm sorry, Grace. Out of order. What you choose to wear and what you choose to drink? Not my business.'

The waiter was approaching with two long cocktails and Nico immediately ordered a glass of fruit juice, but Grace shook her head. His show of sympathy was even more embarrassing than his casual teasing, because that was what it had been. Teasing. Yet somehow it had struck at the very heart of her, had made her feel like a fuddy-duddy, old before her time, and what was worse was the fact that he had a point. That was what life did to a person. That was what *her* life had done to her.

'The cocktail looks wonderful,' she said and the waiter smiled back, flashing white teeth and rattling off a list of enticing ingredients.

'We can eat out here. Appreciate the scenery.' Nico sat back and stared out to the darkening horizon. Fairy lights lit the coconut trees closest to the hotel and beyond the lit trees, darkness was gobbling up everything. The sounds of night insects and frogs and crickets were a background hum, insistent but soothing at the same time.

'It's so beautiful,' Grace murmured. 'Don't you

feel…just a little peaceful sitting out here? Doing nothing?'

'I'm thinking about what we need to do tomorrow. Does that count as *doing nothing*?' But he laughed.

Grace relaxed. It was nice because they were both staring out at the same dark landscape and without his eyes on her she felt less edgy, less self-conscious of the fussy outfit she had chosen to wear. The cocktail looked bright and jolly and harmless, but she could feel the alcohol cutting a path through her reserve, loosening her inhibitions. She sneaked a sideways glance at him and shivered. The light filtering between the shadows and the mellow citronella candles on the tables made him look rakish, like a pirate somehow transported onto solid ground. She gulped and swallowed some more of the cocktail.

'Not really.' She smiled. 'It's strange,' she murmured thoughtfully, 'but when I sit here and look around, when I think of the lanterns in the bar and the wooden counter and all the bright colours everywhere, the picture I have of your uncle doesn't tally with the one you told me about…'

She met his steady gaze when he angled his body so that he was looking at her.

'Am I overstepping the mark?' She raised her eyebrows, finished the cocktail and thought that throwing caution to the wind now and again wasn't half as unnerving as she'd always thought. Frankly, the wind had done quite a bit of caution-devouring over the past week or so. Every time, she had given herself a little lecture on climbing back into her box and re-erecting the barriers between them but just at the moment she honestly didn't feel inclined to do that.

'You're full of surprises of late, Grace Brown, and I have to admit that I'm liking this version,' Nico murmured in a voice that sent little tingles through her because it was as soft as a caress.

'Am I?'

Their eyes tangled.

Nico drew in a sharp breath. Surely his perfect secretary wasn't *flirting* with him?

He dismissed that notion before it had time to take root but as he looked at her now he was struck by just how beautiful she was. Not beautiful in the conventional sense. There was no flamboyance about her, just a quiet intelligence that was far more potent.

How had he not seen that before?

Right now, he could feel her eyes feather over him, and his erection was suddenly as stiff as steel, throbbing and demanding, a physical ache that made him want to push his hand over it to still its insistence.

'You've spent a long time keeping the outspoken side of you under wraps…what's responsible for the sudden volte-face?' He studied her face with leisurely curiosity until he noted the faint pink that crept into her cheeks. 'And why do you say that?'

'Sorry?'

'That this place…doesn't fit the image of the man I painted to you… Explain…'

Grace could feel the rum from the cocktail swimming in her veins. When the waiter approached to offer a refill, she nodded. Two cocktails! Tame by most standards for someone her age!

'You described your uncle as someone…unsavoury, I guess. Out of control and on the wrong side of excess, and yet here…' She looked around her to the wooden banister, smooth from the sun and the salty air, and the hammock to the side and the tasteful clusters of chairs and tables. 'It's so tranquil and atmospheric.' She sighed. 'It's enchanting. In my mind I see a guy who loved the hotel he had started from scratch and everything to do with it, including the bar, which is like a proper fisherman's hang-out. All the art on the walls and the furnishings and the rugs…how could anyone be responsible for all this if he was looking at the world from the bottom of a bottle? And the fishing business—it's been very well run, very tailored to make the most of a commercial market…'

'Which isn't to say that his strenuous efforts to ruin his half of the family business didn't justify his exile to this beautiful island. They did. Sander's race down to the bottom of the gutter wasn't just something that affected *him*. He had no qualms about

dragging hundreds of employees in his hurtle towards self-destruction. So maybe he came here and
managed all this because he knew that he was in the
last-chance saloon. He'd already used up his three
strikes. The choice must have been stark. Ruin his
life here and there would be nowhere left to turn.
People have a way of snapping out of things when
their wriggle room has run out.'

Grace shrugged. 'I suppose...'

'There's no supposing about it.'

No, there wasn't, she thought. She would have
liked to have asked him if that was why he was black
and white when it came to separating work from his
personal life. Two halves never destined to meet,
with his personal life doomed to play second fiddle
to making sure nothing jeopardised the business that
provided an umbrella for so many people.

'You've gone quiet on me,' Nico said drily. He
drained his second cocktail and relaxed back. 'We've
come this far, don't leave me hanging on now...'

He was gazing intently at her face, as if he were
mesmerised by her. The waiter came and he ordered
a cold bottle of wine along with a selection of whatever tapas the chef recommended, and when the
waiter left Nico was leaning into her, having swivelled his chair to face hers.

'Or maybe,' Grace said slowly, 'your uncle, with
all his bad habits, got here and discovered that this
was what was meant to be. He wasn't trapped and
left without a choice.'

'Anyone with a shred of common sense would know to resign themselves to the inevitable and make the best of it.'

'It feels like more than that.' Grace looked around her at the warm surroundings, the old hand-worn sheen of the wooden railings, the little lanterns on the scattered tables, which were attracting small, curious insects, the quirky chimes tinkling in the night breeze. 'It feels like a lot of love went into this hotel and the same with the bar. I haven't seen the fishing fleet yet…'

'*Fleet* is a big word…it's making me think of a large-scale operation instead of a handful of sea-worthy boats with passable equipment on board.' He held his hands up in mock surrender. 'Or am I being a little dismissive here?'

'Okay, maybe not *fleet*. But I'll bet your uncle developed a liking for getting out on the ocean, for fishing.'

Nico gave that some thought. 'I wouldn't know. My father sorted out the business with his brother, sent him out here and I have no idea why this destination was chosen in the first place, and that was the end of the story. If Sander and my father communicated over the years, then those communications were not revealed to me.'

'So your only version was of a dissolute uncle who had to be removed from the damage to the company he was doing and, thanks to your dad, that was what happened…'

'Of course, dead wood must be dealt with,' Nico said coolly. 'You may think that I'm being harsh but, like I said, in the bigger scheme of things, it was what had to be done.'

'I know,' Grace said gently.

'And…?' Nico shifted.

'And what?' Grace shrugged, aware that the conversation had become dangerously intimate, possibly because the alcohol in the cocktails had gone to her head. She had encroached onto his guarded territory and now she anxiously wondered whether he might take offence.

'And you've started this conversation, so don't suddenly start being shy.' He leant forward, his dark eyes glinting with teasing intent. 'You're not playing coy with me, are you? I've always admired your direct approach, and even more now you've decided to clamber out of your shell and peep over the ramparts.'

'Of course I'm not being *coy*,' Grace scoffed, pulling back a bit because his proximity was bringing her out in a cold sweat.

'Don't worry,' Nico purred. 'I'm not suddenly going to start weeping and wailing if you tell me what you think.' He looked at her shrewdly, head tilted to one side. 'And I won't incarcerate you into a nearby dungeon for the crime of speaking your mind,' he added for good measure.

Something feathered through her, setting off warning sparks even though the conversation was light and unthreatening.

Her heart began to beat faster and she licked her lips as nervous tension ramped up, melding into something else, a stirring of excitement that made her want to reach out and close the small distance between them.

Nico's eyes were locked to hers, and he shifted restlessly as the waiter approached, setting up one of the low tables closer to them so that he could arrange the selection of tapas for their enjoyment.

'Say what you have to say,' he murmured huskily. 'I don't bite. Not unless asked.'

Grace sucked in a sharp breath and her eyes widened as she found herself on shifting sands. His eyes...there was a smoky burn in them that made her felt hot and addled. She sifted her fingers through her hair and reached for a plate and a cloth serviette and one of the tapas only to realise that her hand was shaking.

Telling him what she thought would bring this situation back in hand. He didn't like having his walls breached. If she breached them now, then at least it would burst the suffocating tension threading through her, making her feel as though she'd suddenly been plugged into a live socket. Why should she allow him to have fun at her expense?

His irritation would surely be preferable to...to... *this*, whatever *this* was.

'You must have been young when all of this took place.' She took a bite of one of the pastries, which was filled with delicious curry. Her tongue darted out, licking some of the sauce from the side of her mouth. 'Maybe things seemed straightforward then, but if you look at the same situation now you might see things differently.' Another bite of the tapas. It was moreish. 'Aren't you having any? They're delicious.' She reached for another, and just like that she felt the touch of his finger by her mouth and it was electrifying. She couldn't pull away. She couldn't say anything. All she could do was stare at him as he gently wiped something from her mouth.

'Some sauce at the side of your mouth…'

Grace blushed a furious red and wiped where he had touched with the back of her hand. He'd sat back and was staring at her with brooding eyes.

'You were saying?' he asked. He raked his fingers through his hair and glanced away for a few seconds before gazing at her once again.

What had she been saying? Everything had flown out of her head and she had to think hard to remember. Defusing the situation…that was what she'd been aiming to do before he'd sent her thoughts into frantic meltdown by touching her.

'I was saying…' she cleared her throat and dived for another, less tricky tapas '…maybe your uncle was a little wild then he came here and found whatever it was he'd been looking for. Maybe he went off the rails because he didn't know what he wanted from life but here…he found it. You can tell. There's love here. It's in the furnishings and the food and it's there in all the people who worked for him. So he didn't carry on being dissolute. He changed. People do.' She thought of her mother. 'Sometimes.'

'Maybe.' Nico smiled. 'Maybe you have a point. It's not something I've ever considered.'

'I'm sorry if I overstepped the mark but you did ask me to be honest with you.' Grace stared at his mouth, blinked and then found she couldn't tear her eyes away as he reached for an intricate pastry, making far less of a mess of eating it than she had.

'So I did.'

'I hope you're not angry.'

'You veer from spectacular frankness to fawning apology. Grace, we've worked alongside one another for years. You're going to have to find a middle ground that allows you to tell me what's on your mind without being wary of somehow angering me. I'm a big boy. I can deal with whatever you have to throw at me.' He flashed her a killer smile.

He didn't look angry and the killer smile was doing all sorts of things to her body. If she'd planned on diverting him away from whatever he was doing that was heating her up by getting under his skin, then she'd misread the situation. Nico wasn't fazed by her probing. He was fired up by it because, as for her, the buffer zone between them had been removed and he was enjoying himself seeing what had been hiding underneath it. She wasn't getting under his skin. She was amusing him. *He* was the one getting under *her* skin because she was taking all of this seriously.

'So tomorrow…' She reached for something else

and noticed that the cocktail had been replaced with a glass of chilled wine, which she ignored in favour of the bottled water that had been brought to their table.

'Tomorrow?'

'I know we've covered a lot of ground today...' Grace could feel her cheeks getting pinker and pinker as he continued to look at her with an expression she couldn't quite read, an expression that could have been one hundred per cent business or one hundred per cent inappropriate flirting.

'And you have my sincere apologies for that,' Nico returned, pushing his plate to one side with his finger so that he could earnestly lean towards her, his elbows resting on his knees, his hands loosely linked. 'I managed to get things in motion before you arrived, and I figured it might be a good idea to strike while the iron was hot. Get things wrapped up as fast as I could.'

'The employees must be saddened by everything that's happened.'

'They'll get to keep their jobs. I've made it abundantly clear that there will be no sackings.'

'So everything will stay the way it was?'

'That...' Nico frowned '...is not something I can guarantee but why would that be important? Provided they get to keep their jobs, then it'll simply be a change of scenery, so to speak. Of course, if extensive renovations need to be done then I can always write in a clause that protects jobs for the duration.'

'Have you considered that they may have been attached to your uncle? I was chatting to a couple of the guys yesterday who work in the bar and they've been there for ever because they really cared about Sander.'

'They'll recover.'

'Why do you sound so surprised that I'm even asking about this?'

'Because it's just going to be a change of ownership, Grace. Everything else is…emotionalism and I don't have time for any of that.'

'You're so cold, Nico?'

Nico flushed darkly. 'I'm not cold,' he growled, but then he lightened up and sipped some wine. 'You'd be surprised at the number of women who think just the opposite.'

Grace refused to back down even though the heat rushed through her like a torrent. 'I'm sure there are hundreds of them who think just that and have always been more than happy to let you know,' she countered wryly. 'Haven't I dealt with some of them over the years? Crying down the end of the phone, receiving extravagant flowers…because you've decided that you've had enough of them and it's time for your heat to warm someone else up?'

'I always tell the women I date that my heat has a timeline before it burns out. I don't do permanence and I'm upfront about that, so why would I take responsibility for breaking hearts when they've been duly warned to keep their hearts intact?'

'That's not what I'm talking about, Nico.'

They stared at one another and Grace met his gaze steadily, and, with a barely contained sigh of impatience, eventually he shrugged.

'I know,' he muttered gruffly. He huffed an exaggerated sigh. 'Okay. You win.'

'Sorry?'

He smiled and raised both hands in a gesture of surrender. His smile was so sincere, so oddly boyish that for a few seconds Grace felt the ground move under her feet and she expelled one long, shaky breath. She was seeing behind the façade that could be so charming and yet so remote at the same time. He lowered his eyes and her heart flip-flopped inside her.

'I'll...talk to them. Listen to what they have to say instead of...'

'Treating them like chess pieces to be manoeuvred into place?'

Nico grinned, burst out laughing and then said, with laughter still in his voice, 'Is that how you think I treat people?'

'When it comes to business, yes.'

'Never got chess. I don't think I ever had the patience to sit it out.'

'That's a shame because you're probably a natural.' She could have added that the way he treated women was hardly any different, but she knew he would have been offended because, in his eyes, he was the soul of generosity. He was capable of lavishing everything on the woman he dated and what he'd just said confirmed what she had always suspected. He was a commitment-phobe who entered relationships with no intention of any of those relationships outstaying their welcome, and that was just fine because he was a decent guy who laid his cards on the table from the very start.

But she felt a small sense of victory that he would chat to Sander's employees, who would all have some kind of story to tell, she suspected. It would be a shame if he left with that one-dimensional picture of his uncle still ingrained in his head. She ruefully thought that she might have had a bit of a life, been a bit more selfish with her choices, if she'd been able to see her mother as a one-dimensional figure instead of someone lovable but flawed, a parent in need of parenting herself and with a daughter all too willing to take on the role.

'But we were talking about tomorrow.' Grace returned to the safe topic of work. 'I can transcribe everything discussed at the meetings today and have them ready for you by tomorrow.'

'Very efficient.'

'I can actually head in now and get started?'

'That's efficiency beyond the call of duty, Grace.'

'Isn't that why I'm here?'

'Today was full on. Yes, you're here to work but I'm not a slave driver and I'm guessing that you haven't been to this part of the world before. Have you?'

'Well, no,' Grace answered awkwardly.

'Thought not. So you were asking about tomorrow? Time off.'

'I beg your pardon?'

'You're going to have a little time off to enjoy the island. It's very beautiful.'

Grace smiled slowly, too thrilled by that suggestion to press her case for doing what she was being paid to do.

'I have a driver at hand and at our disposal.'

Her smile slipped a little. 'That sounds wonderful.'

'I need to be in town so we can head off first thing in the morning and I insist above everything else...' he leaned towards her and said in a low, conspiratorial voice '...that you visit some of the shops. The choice might be limited but you should find more suitable attire there.' He leant back and waved one hand. '*Not*,' he stressed with vigour, 'that I'm telling you what to wear. Like I said, far be it from me to dictate your choice of clothing. That would be downright tyranny. But if you've just come equipped with stuff you'd wear to work in London on a mild summer day, then you're going to be very uncomfortable in this heat while we're here. And before you say anything...it's all on the company. After all, you're only here because of me.'

FREE BOOKS GIVEAWAY

YOU pick your books –
WE pay for everything.
You get up to FOUR New Books and TWOMystery Gifts...absolutely FREE!

Dear Reader,

I am writing to announce the launch of a huge **FREE BOOK GIVEAWAY**... and to let you know that YOU are entitled to choose up to FOUR fantastic books that WE pay for.

Try **Harlequin® Desire** books featuring the worlds of the American elite with juicy plot twists, delicious sensuality and intriguing scandal.

Try **Harlequin Presents® Larger-Print** books featuring the glamourous lives of royals and billionaires in a world of exotic locations, where passion knows no bounds.

Or **TRY BOTH!**

In return, we ask just one favor: Would you please participate in our brief Reader Survey? We'd love to hear from you.

This FREE BOOKS GIVEAWAY means that your introductory shipment is completely free, <u>even the shipping</u>! If you decide to continue, you can look forward to curated monthl shipments of brand-new books from your selected series, always at a discount off the cover price! <u>Plus you can cance any time</u>. Who could pass up a deal like that?

Sincerely

Pam Powers

Pam Powers
For Harlequin Reader Servic

Complete the survey below and return it today to receive up to 4 FREE BOOKS and FREE GIFTS guaranteed!

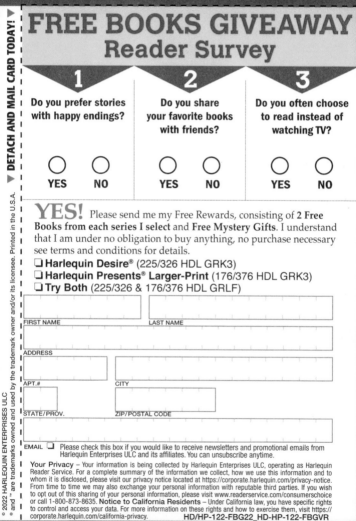

DETACH AND MAIL CARD TODAY!

FREE BOOKS GIVEAWAY
Reader Survey

1

Do you prefer stories with happy endings?

◯ YES ◯ NO

2

Do you share your favorite books with friends?

◯ YES ◯ NO

3

Do you often choose to read instead of watching TV?

◯ YES ◯ NO

YES! Please send me my Free Rewards, consisting of **2 Free Books from each series I select** and **Free Mystery Gifts.** I understand that I am under no obligation to buy anything, no purchase necessary see terms and conditions for details.

❑ **Harlequin Desire®** (225/326 HDL GRK3)
❑ **Harlequin Presents® Larger-Print** (176/376 HDL GRK3)
❑ **Try Both** (225/326 & 176/376 HDL GRLF)

FIRST NAME

LAST NAME

ADDRESS

APT.#

CITY

STATE/PROV.

ZIP/POSTAL CODE

EMAIL ❑ Please check this box if you would like to receive newsletters and promotional emails from Harlequin Enterprises ULC and its affiliates. You can unsubscribe anytime.

HD/HP-122-FBG22_HD-HP-122-FBGVR

© 2022 HARLEQUIN ENTERPRISES ULC
® and ™ are trademarks owned and used by the trademark owner and/or its licensee. Printed in the U.S.A.

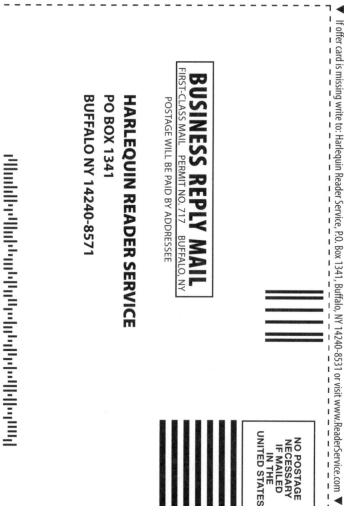

CHAPTER SIX

NESTLED AMIDST THE swaying coconut trees and cut into an irregular clearing was the hotel swimming pool. It was small, but then so was the hotel, and was thoughtfully designed to blend in with the surroundings. Instead of the usual blue-tiled bottom and scattering of deck chairs, it was shaped to mimic a natural body of water, with a small, gurgling waterfall at one end and shallow steps carved to resemble a smooth, rocky incline down into the green, still water.

It was five in the evening, still light but with the sun beginning to dip, and it was certainly still hot. Humid and muggy and without the slightest whisper of a breeze.

Even the usual orchestra of insects seemed to have gone into hiding.

Nico was listening, the general manager talking to him, his voice low and urgent, but his eyes were absently on the figure in the swimming pool.

When he had airily told his secretary to have a

day off, to enjoy the town, the scenery, the extraordinary beauty of the place and to think about buying herself some more appropriate clothing, he had half expected her to ignore everything he'd said. Years of working closely together had taught him that, underneath the controlled exterior, Grace had a mind of her own and, when it came to non-work-related issues, she would do precisely what she wanted to do even if she remained ultra-polite as she dug her heels in.

Being here on the island had confirmed that suspicion, had made him realise just how much fire burned beneath the cool, composed surface.

But she had done as asked. She had taken a few hours off two days ago, had explored the town with his driver at her disposal, had gone to a couple of the beaches on her own and had visited the limited supply of shops where she had bought…yes…more suitable attire.

Colours. Stuff that wasn't in varying shades of bland. Light, colourful clothes far better suited to the searing heat, which not even the overhead fans in the conference room of the hotel in the town they had used for meetings could temper.

The swimsuit, he noted as he continued to gaze in her direction, had sadly and clearly remained the original one she had brought with her. A black one-piece ideally suited for no-nonsense competitive swimming. Nothing frivolous there.

Yet she was still so crazily sexy in the damned

thing that Nico was having trouble focusing on what Steve, the general manager, was saying.

He wasn't sure whether it was the fact that they were not in their normal habitat or whether it was because he was seeing sides of her for the first time that tantalised him, or whether it was a mixture of both, but he was finding his concentration slip far too often for his liking.

Eyes drifting to the slight push of her breasts against her light cotton tee shirt...thoughts turning to what lay underneath that light cotton tee shirt... and dreams in which disjointed images of her made for restless sleep.

He tore his eyes away with some difficulty and firmly focused on the matter in hand.

'Look at the sky.' Steve gave a curt nod in the direction of the indigo blue yonder and Nico frowned.

'I agree it seems more humid than it has been for the past few days...'

'You need to know this part of the world, Mr Doukas, sir, to see the signs. Hurricane coming. No announcement yet, but we know how to read the signs. Not just the humidity, Mr Doukas, but you hear this silence? The insects gone into hiding.'

As far as Nico could see, nothing much was that different, but he was willing to bow to greater local knowledge and, after fifteen minutes, he walked towards the swimming pool, towards Grace, who was doing lengths, her slender body cleaving through the water with surprising speed.

He stooped by the side of the pool. There was no decking. Instead, the pool was built into the earth so his loafers sank a little into the damp grass that inclined down. He watched her swim to him, oblivious of his presence as he waited for her, and he noted the widening of her eyes as she abruptly stopped and clung to the side.

'Oh. Hi.'

Grace had sneaked out to the inviting pool, very much aware that she was overreacting because even if Nico was around, even if he was sitting on one of the rattan chairs dotted in the beautiful clearing under the shade of one of the trees, there was no reason for her to be uncomfortable.

The day had been non-stop. They had gone from hotel to offices and at lunch time had interrupted the schedule with a private plane to Nassau so that they could get signatures on paper for the fishing business. She was exhausted.

That said, she had been relieved when Nico had told her that he planned on carrying on with some bits and pieces in the manager's office at the hotel, which he'd had adapted to use as their on-site office.

But he was here now, and she felt exposed as she trod water. 'I thought you were working,' she said a little breathlessly.

'I was until Steve showed up. You need to come to the office. There's a situation.'

'What? What situation? What's going on?'

'I'll wait for you inside. Don't be long and…apologies for spoiling the party and dragging you out of the pool. I realise it's been a hellishly long day for us.'

Grace watched as he vaulted upright, his expression thoughtful, before striding off back towards the hotel. It was so unusual for Nico to reveal any sign of urgency about anything, however stressful things might be, that her heart was pounding with anxiety as she hurried out of the pool towards the office to meet him.

Should she go change? She slipped on the cotton shorts she had worn over the swimsuit and slung her towel over her shoulders.

The hotel had gradually shed more of its guests, people whose time there had come to an end and hadn't been replaced with new intake, so there were relatively few people around. She headed straight for the manager's office to find Nico standing with his back to the door, staring out of the window, and he didn't immediately look around when she entered, not until she coughed, at which point he slowly turned to face her, face grave.

'Sit down, Grace.'

'What's going on? Has the sale fallen through? Is there an emergency back home? Are your parents okay?'

'I've just been speaking to Steve. Look, this is going to be a long conversation. You should probably go change out of your wet swimsuit.'

'I just want to know what's happening. You're stressing me out.'

'Don't tell me that's new on you.' But his wry humour was forced. 'And here I was thinking how well you've always managed stress, because that was one of the clauses in your contract when I hired you. Steve has told me that rumours are swirling of a hurricane on the way. There has been no announcement yet, but he says everyone on the island can predict a landfall hurricane by a change in the atmosphere. It would seem the atmosphere has changed. When he pointed it out, it did occur to me that there's something heavy in the air today. Have you felt it?'

'It's been a bit sticky.'

'If he's right, then there are going to be some change to our plans.'

'What do you mean?'

'The timeline was for our return no later than tomorrow evening. Enough has been put in place for me to delegate the remaining detail to the lawyers and accountants who have been working on things in Nassau. If a hurricane is en route, then we can try to accelerate the last few changes that need to be cemented into the contracts or else we evacuate now, today, and return at a later date. Failing either of those options, we might just have to ride things out, which means possibly being stranded here for longer than anticipated.'

'Stranded?' Grace thought of Tommy worriedly.

'Problems there?' Nico looked at her narrowly,

his antenna picking up more than just routine concern, nudging his curiosity and reminding him of the
hidden depths he had glimpsed swirling beneath the
unrevealing, predictable façade.

'I have commitments…er…back at home.'

'What commitments?'

'The usual.' Grace shrugged. He had told her
things about himself, or rather about his background,
but sharing wasn't in his nature, and she had no intention of sharing her own troubles with Tommy or
anything about her complicated background. This
wasn't because she felt he would not be sympathetic,
but some gut instinct warned her that that level of
confidence would not be welcome. Not in any way,
shape or form.

'It's more than possible that there won't be any
hurricane. These things develop out at sea and their
path can be erratic and tricky to predict but just in
case…'

A lot to do.

That, Grace discovered nearly an hour later, was
the upshot. The remaining guests at the hotel were
briefed and told that they could choose to stay put
because there was no certainty of anything happening, or else they could be transferred to whatever
hotel in Nassau they wanted at no personal cost. Or
flights back to the USA could be arranged immediately, as they were all from various parts of America.

Five couples and none with kids as they were all

elderly, enjoying the freedom of children having flown the nest.

There was remarkably little dithering and, by evening, all had packed and left the hotel for a trip back to the USA, largely because their stays were pretty much finishing anyway.

Grace personally felt that it was all much ado about nothing, because there was not so much as a drop of rain or ominous roll of thunder.

Nico removed himself to the office to power through a series of emails and she enjoyed the evening to herself, sitting on the sprawling wooden veranda that circled the hotel like a bracelet, watching fireflies and listening to the rolling of waves on the shore.

This was the most removed she had ever felt in her life from her problems. Even Tommy, whose welfare was constantly on her mind, seemed more distant, and from this distance, with the slim possibility of not being able to return to London at the scheduled time, she wondered whether her unforeseen absence might not do him good.

For the first time she really thought about the implications of having spent a lifetime mothering him. All those years when Cecily had been missing in action and then, seamlessly, picking up the baton when he had had his accident, when Cecily had cheerfully waved goodbye and vanished to the other side of the world with her new husband.

Had she made Tommy over-dependent on her?

She spoke to him most evenings in London, went to see him sometimes as often as twice a week. She had been given permission by him to talk to his therapist about sessions and she did. With regularity. As with his various physios. She was ever present, concerned and encouraging. But had that concern and encouragement stopped her brother from taking responsibility for himself? Had it stopped her from taking responsibility for herself? For a future still waiting in the wings to get going? Had she carved a role for herself and cemented herself in, only willing to indulge a crush on her boss that would never come to anything? Had it been easier to do nothing rather than break free of her cage? One Internet date that hadn't worked out and she had once again retreated from doing what needed to be done to really build a life for herself. And maybe, by focusing so much on Tommy, she had also taken away his independence and his need to build a life for *himself*.

Only here in these peaceful surroundings had she really thought about that.

Grace only noticed the sudden stillness when she heard a very distant rumble of thunder.

It was so far away that she didn't give it a second thought, but she woke when it was still dark, in the early hours of the morning, to a banging on her door, and when she pulled it open, rubbing her eyes drowsily, it was to find Nico standing in the doorway. He looked dishevelled.

'The hurricane warning came through a couple

of hours ago. The meteorologists were convinced that it was going to veer away, straight towards the east coast of America, but it unexpectedly swerved, hence the late, frantic warning.' He raked his fingers through his hair and looked at her with piercing dark eyes.

'What time is it?'

'After eight.'

'What?'

'It's pitch-black outside even though it's morning.' He strode past her to pull back the curtains and the shutters before turning to look at her. 'I've been up dragging anything that could move to safer quarters.'

'You should have got me up!'

Nico was in a pair of jeans and a tee shirt, which belatedly drew her attention to her attire, an oversized tee shirt and nothing else. Bare feet. A pair of lacy knickers under the tee shirt. Underneath her always sober practical clothes she had always worn sexy underwear. She wrapped her arms around herself and as she walked towards him the sudden crack of thunder was so sharp and so dramatic that she physically jumped.

Sudden panic bloomed inside her.

Nico dropped the wooden shutters, plunging the room into a twilight darkness before turning on the standing light.

'The winds are going to gather pace,' he said curtly. 'It's important to stay away from the windows. Don't be tempted to look out because the window panes might shatter under the force of the wind. And don't, under any circumstances, venture outside to see what's happening.' He frowned. 'You look terrified.'

Grace gulped and then jumped again at another crack of thunder and then the sound of rain, racing along the walls and on the roof, as ferocious as the sound of a thundering waterfall. She felt as though the entire structure of the building was going to cave in.

And the temperature seemed to have dropped. Or was that her imagination? She couldn't move a muscle.

'I'm fine,' she breathed, her voice staccato with fear. She could hear the unexpectedly loud sound of the gale gathering strength, could almost feel it battering against the hotel walls, desperate to find a way in so that it could sweep everything away in its destructive path.

They were in this hotel on their own because the few remaining guests had been dispatched to safety and the employees had been sent to their own homes to batten down the hatches.

She stepped towards Nico. She was barely aware of doing so.

She cried out when thunder ripped through the room again and lightning flashed as bright as a sudden blaze of fire.

And just like that, several things happened at once. She moved at the same time as her boss, fear meeting strength, panic rushing into the arms of calm, and he enfolded her.

Everything faded. The howling of the wind…the clatter of rain…the terrifying darkness of day that had suddenly turned to night.

Grace held onto him. Her arms snaked around his whipcord-lean body and she felt the hardness of muscle pressed against her, strong and comforting.

His clothes rasped against her almost but not quite naked body. Her breasts were squashed against his chest but she could still feel the tightness of her nipples blooming at the contact, tingling, making her want to whimper.

'Are you?' Nico husked, tilting her chin so that their eyes met. 'Fine?'

'I will be.' Grace couldn't look away. Her breath was catching in her throat and just getting those words out was an effort. She was no longer the efficient secretary always in control and, even though part of her knew that she should be doing her best to return to that person, right now that felt more like an aspiration than reality. Reality was *this*. 'I… I'm scared…'

Nico felt her vulnerability and it went to him like a shot of adrenaline.

Fire and ice…remote yet direct…strong yet vulnerable. All her complexities lent her a sexiness that might have been latent before, a tantalising suggestion lying just beneath the surface, but here and now they coalesced into something irresistible although he continued to fight it, common sense struggling to win the battle, even as he lowered his dark head, his lips searching for hers.

He kissed her. The second his mouth found hers, anything gentle disappeared under the force of an eroticism that knocked him sideways.

He tasted her hungrily, greedily, his tongue pushing into her mouth and his arms tightening their grip so that he could feel every bit of her pressed against him.

A hurricane was whipping into a frenzy outside and yet all Nico was aware of was the meshing of their tongues and the feel of her peachy bottom as he cupped it in his big hands.

She wanted him.

Was it just fear of the elements that had thrown her into a temporary state of recklessness? Had it blurred the lines between them to the point where she was reacting in a way she would regret? Would the scrabbling slide of her fingers trying to find a way to his bare skin retreat in horror the minute the rain eased off?

Nico knew that any hint of regret, any passing thought that he might have taken advantage of an unusual situation, would be anathema to him and he detached from her with effort but didn't release her, just lightened his hold.

'I want you, Grace,' he said in a driven undertone. 'And it's not just...' he nodded vaguely to encompass the room although his eyes didn't leave her face '…the hurricane outside making me behave out of character. *I want you.* What I *don't* want is for you to fall into my arms because you're scared and then, when you're no longer scared, you somehow throw the blame on my shoulders.' Nico raked his fingers through his hair. 'Tell me to stop,' he grated, his voice barely audible over the shrieking of the weather, 'and I'll stop. Immediately. And never again will this happen or be mentioned. It will have been a…temporary, fleeting blip.'

Grace shivered. Her mouth was still tingling from his and she could still taste him. It felt surreal because this was what she had fantasised about for such a long time. Fantasy had somehow become reality and if in her wildest dreams she had felt her body burn at his touch, it was nothing compared to the reality of what she was feeling now. As though she was alive, lit from within, every sense heightened to a point where she could scarcely credit that this was *her*, Grace Brown, whose life had always been so cautiously lived.

Between her legs was a fierce itch that made her want to rub them together.

Made her want him to touch her down there, to stroke until the itch was gone.

He would back away.

She just had to come to her senses, but she didn't want to come to her senses. She wasn't a fool, and she knew just what her boss was like, where his limitations lay. No commitment. Suited her. Physical attraction, an inappropriate crush, didn't turn her into a complete idiot. She was no more likely to want involvement with Nico than he would want it with her.

Maybe not for the same reasons but all the same. The net result amounted to the same thing.

And in the meantime?

'Right now,' she breathed huskily, 'I want you, Nico. I don't...want you to stop and I'm not going to blame you for anything. I know you for who you are and, trust me, I'm not going to want more than what's happening between us right here and right now. No tomorrow, just today.' She cupped the thick brown column of his neck with her hand, marvelling at how pale she was in comparison.

She had forgotten what it felt like to live in the moment because the business of fretting about tomorrow had always taken precedence. It felt heady.

She tentatively wriggled her fingers under the waistband of his trousers and his low moan went to her head like incense.

He propelled her back, small steps at a time until her knees buckled against the edge of the mattress.

Half laughing, half serious because the howling winds made for an incongruous situation, she asked him whether they should be doing something.

'Other than this?' Nico growled, standing up to strip off his tee shirt in one swift motion.

Headiness was making breathing laborious. He

towered at the side of the bed, a monument to sheer physical perfection, from the arrogant beauty of his face to the bronzed muscularity of his body.

She gasped as he hooked his finger at the zip of his trousers. She could discern the bulge of his erection and for a few seconds she closed her eyes to get a grip.

'You can look now,' Nico husked, and she opened one eye then both, propping herself on her elbows and then downright staring because he was completely naked. His fingers lightly circled his penis, and he absently played with himself while his eyes remained on her face, wickedly amused and dark with intent.

'Like what you see?' he murmured, closing the small gap between them so that he was standing right next to her. 'Because now it's my turn and I'm not going to help. I want to see you get undressed. I want to savour every second of the sight.'

His desire was boldly stamped in his dark eyes and it acted as a spur, so that she stripped off in record time, alive to him in a way that made her daydreams feel like girlish nonsense.

He rifled blindly for the wallet in his trousers to extract a condom, but she stopped him, huskily telling him that she was on the pill.

In a mad moment of moving forward with her life and going on the Internet to find her soulmate, she had done what was necessary and gone on the pill because there was no way she would get herself into any kind of situation where she might be dependent on someone else taking responsibility for an outcome that would enormously and directly affect *her*.

She was realistic enough to know that while she would rather sleep with a guy if she was assured of a positive outcome, that was just not how life worked.

She'd never imagined that the guy she ended up in bed with might be her boss.

He was lowering himself onto the mattress next to her. She had wriggled up to the pillows without realising it and as the mattress depressed under his weight she curved to face him, bodies pressing hot against one another. Outside the driving rain continued its furious attack, pelting against the building, driven by the gale-force winds. Yet here, in the room, Grace was only aware of Nico and the demands of her body, coming alive to remind her that she was still young and with sexual needs that yearned to be satisfied.

She ran her hand experimentally along his waist, along his thigh and then inwards, tremulously feeling the bristle of his hair as she touched the heavy sacs and then the erection pulsing between them.

She wanted to pass out.

She was so wet for him. The taste of this forbidden fruit was so dangerously sweet. She slid her fingers along his shaft and he groaned again, covering her hand with his, stopping her, telling her that it was too much.

'Want me to come?' he joked but his voice was

shaky. He cupped her breast and then straddled her, paying attention to the delicate mound that had occupied way too much of his imagination of late. Perfectly shaped, a handful and just about, the pink nipple a perfect disc and swollen with arousal.

He lowered himself to take one nipple into his mouth and its nectar sweetness sent his heated libido into the stratosphere. He suckled on it, licking and rolling his tongue over the stiffened bud while his fingers moved over her flat belly until they found the soft hair at the juncture between her thighs. He slid one finger lower, and Grace let her thighs fall open so that he could insert his finger. He moved it inside her until she was panting and then, with just the right amount of pressure, he gently grooved it over her clitoris and Grace loosed a low groan of pleasure.

Assailed on both fronts, mouth and hands driving her into a frenzy of desire, she could feel herself hurtling towards the edge and weakly tried to regain some control because she wanted him inside her. She didn't want to come against his questing finger even though her body was on a trajectory that made it hard to resist.

She curled her fingers into his hair and tugged and he obediently unlatched from her nipple but only to torment her more by trailing his tongue over her stomach, finding her belly button and briefly stopping to explore the indent before moving further downwards.

By the time Nico was finally inside her, he had taken her body to heights she had never dreamed possible.

He had teased and licked and drawn sighs and gasps and utterances from her that had sounded alien to her ears.

Fantasy and reality had merged into a crescendo of pent-up longing that was as overpowering as a tsunami. Wrapped up in her little cocoon, plodding the same path every day, Grace was ripe for just the sort of response Nico so effortlessly provoked.

She came almost as soon as he began thrusting deep into her, losing herself in sensation, all self-control abandoned as her body soared towards an orgasm that wrenched a sob of utter satisfaction and fulfilment from her.

Only when they were lying, spent, did Grace wake up to the weather happening outside.

She glanced towards the window and the sliver of grey light struggling to get past the shutters.

'What are we going to do?' she whispered. 'How long do you think this is going to last?'

Nico had to drag his sluggish brain back to Planet Earth because his body was still lazily luxuriating in a post-coital glow he had never experienced in his life before.

Who knew breaking with routine could feel so good?

He didn't want to talk about the prosaic stuff

about what happened next or how long the filthy weather was going to last. For once, practicalities weren't demanding his immediate attention even though, given the situation, they should have been.

Nico thought that what he really wanted to do was stay right where he was, with Grace curled against him, letting the heat subside before stoking it all over again. He had been satisfied, mind-blowingly so, and yet he wanted more.

She was gazing at him with a frown. Why was she so anxious about how long they might be trapped by the weather? Did a couple of extra days here throw everything out of sync for her? She was dependent-free and would have been in the office in London anyway. And besides...shouldn't she be yearning to be marooned here with him? After the mind-blowing experience they had just shared? A keen sense of self-irony made him smile at his own over-inflated ego.

'No idea,' he murmured truthfully, distracted by her sweet, newly made-love-to scent. 'The actual hurricane might just last a day or so but that doesn't mean we're going to be heading back to London as soon as it's blown over.'

'Why not?'

'Because...' The *shouldn't-you-want-to-prolong this?* crazy notion side-swiped him again, leaving a sour aftertaste because it smacked of a lack of self-control on his part. 'Because there will be a lot of destruction left in the wake of the hurricane. Trees blown over...damage no doubt to property. We will be fine here because this is a well-constructed hotel, but I have no doubt there will be time needed to clear debris and, of course, the airstrip will doubtless be affected.' He paused and said evenly, 'So if you've made plans in the next week or so, then I'd advise you to think again.'

'*A week or so?*'

'It's not a lifetime in the great scheme of things.' Nico was astounded that he was the one promoting a laid-back approach when his life was so tailored to put work first.

He felt her stiffen and wondered what she was thinking. How was it that she could writhe with such abandon in his arms and yet withdraw into herself the way he felt she was doing now?

And why did he care?

He propped himself on one elbow then slid off the side of the bed to pad towards the window, doing the very thing he had advised against but needing to get his thoughts in order.

He slid apart the wooden shutters and there, in all its glory, was proof of what he had just said. A hurricane wreaking havoc. The trees were bending at right angles, whipped this way and that by the gale-force winds. Plants had been ripped from beds, flowers torn from hedges and the sky was dark with rage.

A few more days…

She might be anxious. God knew, she might have commitments she didn't want to cancel…but as far as he was concerned?

His body was still on fire for her and a few more days cooped up here was certainly not giving him pause for thought.

It should have been, but it wasn't and, for the first time in years, Nico was disturbed by the grey area where things weren't as clear-cut as he'd want them to be.

But who safer for a brief fling with here than his secretary? She knew him well enough to know that, once they left this island, whatever they'd shared would be relegated to the history books. She knew him for the man he was.

No need for warning speeches, no need to be on the lookout for clinginess, no hinting that a future might lie with someone on a distant horizon.

Just…sex.

Nico turned to smile at her. She might be concerned but he was confident that he would be able to change her mind and make her see that a few days here might just be fun.

CHAPTER SEVEN

GRACE KNEW THAT what she was doing was a dangerous indulgence. What they were *both* doing.

Taking time out from reality. Having glorious sex
as though they were a couple of frisky teenagers
without a care in the world.

Instead of a thirty-one-year-old woman and her
out-of-bounds, sexy-as-hell boss.

The hurricane had swept through, leaving behind
a trail of destruction and, yes, the small airport had
been out of commission for two days, but it was now
up and running, yet she and Nico were still here, and
the only place *they* were running to was the bedroom,
so that they could lose themselves in wild, crazy
passion.

Of course, work continued. Of course she still
went through his emails and arranged his conference calls and participated in various Zoom meetings concerning deals coming to fruition.

The difference? The prissy outfits were gone, as
were the ramparts she had studiously erected to pro-

tect herself against the inconvenient attraction she'd kept under wraps for years. There were no busy eyes in an office that had to be avoided. Out here, they had complete freedom to do whatever they wanted to and what they wanted to do was touch one another.

He stroked her inner leg as he chatted on the airwaves to company directors scattered across the globe. He reached to cup her wetness, his hand moving rhythmically against her panties as he finalised the details about the sale of the hotel and the bar and the fishing business. Only yesterday, as he had lounged on the leather sofa in Steve's office, with her next to him and the computer winking in front, he had lazily slipped his finger underneath her dress and inserted it with devastating efficiency into her wetness. She had zoned out from the conversation he had been having with one of his CEOs on the telephone, which had been on speaker. As he had stroked the engorged slit between her thighs, she had done the unthinkable and spasmed against his finger, barely able to contain her urge to scream out her satisfaction, acutely conscious of the business discussion taking place. He had shot her a wicked smile, mouthed *Have you had fun?* and she had felt her body go up in flames, mortified and blisteringly excited at the same time.

When they were in the company of other people, when they were dealing with various employees, they were the soul of discretion but once those doors were closed behind them, they couldn't keep their hands off one another.

Of course, it was going to come to an end. That was a given. There had been no need for him to tell her because she knew him well enough to know where his flings led and what they had here, in this bubble, wasn't even a fling.

It was more a weakness to which they had both succumbed...a fleeting moment in time soon to be papered over by a return to routine.

Grace didn't know when that return was coming, and she had shied away from asking because she was having fun. For the first time in her life, she was having fun. Was it so wrong to want to prolong this forbidden situation? She would return to London and head straight back to life on the straight and narrow. Meanwhile, Tommy seemed content enough to manage without her, but by the time she went to see him he would be back to his usual self, dissatisfied and querulous and in need of guidance. That being the case, she would be a saint not to want to snatch this stolen pleasure.

Sitting on the wide porch, to which the outside furniture had been returned from the spacious shed that was used for storage in bad weather, Grace drew her knees up to her chest and watched the distant figure in the ocean. It was a little after six and after a day of meetings, calls and the usual tidying of the beach area, Nico was striking back from his ocean swim.

He was a powerful swimmer, had laughed at her concern the first time he had sauntered down to the water's edge and plunged straight into the bright blue sea.

He liked swimming at night. She could feel the build of excitement as he sliced through the water, getting closer and closer.

They had become accustomed to having the hotel to themselves. It was small and cosy, and the employees had been only too glad to be relieved of their duties, not that they were overworked because, aside from the two of them, the place was empty.

The solitude lent itself to all sorts of titillating situations and Grace shivered with pleasure just thinking about them.

Four days felt like four weeks because time seemed to stand still out here.

She straightened as Nico emerged from the water, rearing up from the softly breaking waves like a monolith.

He paused to sweep his fingers through his wet hair and then, eyes locked to her, headed in her direction, a dark silhouette in the fast-fading light.

He stopped just in front of her and then leant down, hands firmly planted on the arms of her chair, caging her in.

'You should try some night swimming with me,' he murmured.

'I don't think so.' Grace smiled back at him and then curled her finger into a wayward strand of dark hair. 'I'm too much of a coward, I'm afraid.'

'What's to be afraid of? When you'd be swimming next to me?'

'Oh, right. I forgot. Nothing would dare attack if they sensed that you were in the water...'

'Correct.' Nico leant into her, kissed her long and slow until her eyelids were fluttering and the ache between her legs made her brain shut down the way it always seemed to. 'Besides, you swim like a fish. Whoever taught at school did a good job.'

He grinned. In response, Grace said nothing. She'd never had swimming lessons at school. They had been an adult treat at the local swimming baths. She could have told him but what they had did not include intimate sharing of confidences. He had admitted to his uncle's past because it had formed the backdrop for their trip to the island. Grace had savoured that titbit, but she had not returned the favour and nor would she.

Nico walked alone. Any girlish desire to share secrets about herself would send him into rapid retreat because it would make him think that she might be reading a depth to what they had that wasn't there and never would be.

In essence, she was his loyal secretary who had stepped outside the box for a moment in time.

He knew nothing about her background and nothing about her circumstances and he hadn't asked.

He hadn't asked because this was about sex. When it came to knowing *her*, he knew enough. He knew that she was reliable and did a good job and knew how to take the initiative at work when she had to.

The fact that he had caught her on an Internet date had opened a door between them, but this was where that open door had led to. Great sex.

Yet, if this was just lust, then why did he fill her head every waking moment? If she didn't care, why was there a sneaking suspicion that she would be hurt by all of this? If she really thought that by sleeping with him, she might get him out of her system, then why did the thought of losing him fill her with dread? Why did the prospect of returning to normality, picking up where they had left off, pretending that nothing had happened between them, fill her with panic?

Because she was falling for him? How could that be possible when it made no sense?

For Grace, whose life had always made sense, who had mastered the art of turning chaos into order, the recklessness of falling for Nico Doukas brought her out in a cold sweat.

Even more terrifying was the thought that he might somehow wise up to what she was feeling.

What if he saw past the shiny veneer to the murky, muddy confusion underneath?

What he didn't know about women could be written on the back of a postage stamp. How long before she let something slip, let her feelings for him show on her face…? Then what? He would be horrified. As far as Nico was concerned, they were on the same page. Some unexpected fun in the sun, a break from routine. She knew him, as he was fond of reminding her. She knew the man he was and the one he could never be.

She knew the rules of the game.

The slightest whiff that she had strayed from following those rules and everything would be lost. There was no way he would keep her on because she would risk becoming an embarrassing and needy liability. He would no longer be able to look her in the face and the relationship they had built up over the years would be gone for ever.

'Things…seem to be progressing really well… here… I know we've had to stay here longer than originally planned because of the hurricane but I've been surprised at how efficient everyone is when it comes to tidying up behind it.'

'They're used to it. Hurricanes happen every year here. A lot of the places, as you've seen, are built in ways that withstand the onslaught.'

Grace was temporarily distracted. She looked at him with curious eyes.

'What did it feel like?'

'Come again?'

'Helping clear the beach…all the debris…sorting out rebuilding some of those houses that were battered. Have you ever done anything like that before?'

'That's a very serious question,' Nico murmured, flinging himself on the beach towel spread next to hers and lying on his back, hands folded on his broad chest.

'Oh, sorry. I forgot that we steered clear of serious questions.'

'Have I ever said that?' He angled himself so that he was looking at her.

'Nico, you don't have to.' Grace laughed lightly. 'And it wasn't a serious question. It was just…a question.'

'To answer you,' Nico said pensively, after a few seconds of telling silence, 'yes and no. The physical exertion felt good. I've never been called on to do anything like that before. There was never any need. No need, growing up, to earn some money by working on a building site during the summer holidays. No need to go fruit picking to grab a bit of freedom.' He was staring up at the twilit sky again.

'Oh, the headache of growing up in a rich family.'

'What about you?'

'Normal.' Grace thought of her far from normal background and wondered what he would make of it.

'Is there ever such a thing?'

The conversation was beginning to feel dangerous, like suddenly staring down into an open fire.

'Of course there is!' She laughed. 'It's getting a little chilly out here.'

She rose and he did as well to begin drying himself with the towel he had been lying on.

'It is.' He spun round to face her, his dark gaze hot with lazy, sexy amusement. 'I have a number of options when it comes to warming you up.' He feathered his finger across her cheek and for a few seconds her head emptied of all intent as her body revved up in expectation of more.

He dipped his finger over her lips then into her parted mouth and Grace went weak at the knees. She sucked it, their eyes locked, her body melting. When he curved his hand to cup the side of her neck and drew her towards him, she didn't resist.

She edged closer, weaved her arms around his neck and pulled him down to press her mouth against his, to savour the wetness of his tongue meshing with hers and to enjoy all the attendant reactions that lingering kiss roused in her.

She would get a grip. The control she'd given up was waiting to be regained. She'd seen the danger in front of her and had known what steps had to be taken to limit the damage that would be caused.

She would save herself but first...

Would it be a crime to take what was on offer one last time? Wouldn't that just be playing him at his own game? When it came to women and from everything Grace had ever seen, Nico took what he wanted. Why shouldn't she take what *she* wanted? Would one more day make a broken heart more difficult to mend?

Because she would have a broken heart. She had made the fatal mistake of giving it to the wrong guy and there would be a heavy price to pay for her misguided generosity.

How ironic to think that she had watched her mother's shenanigans, had resolved to make sure never to go down a similar road of losing her heart willy-nilly in a frantic search for validation from a guy, only to find herself, at the age of thirty-one, so naive that she had gone and done the very thing she had spent a lifetime cautioning herself about.

In hindsight, she could have used some of her mother's experience when it came to playing the field because she might have been better at protecting herself from Nico and the consequences of falling for him.

Grace felt as though the weight of her poor choices would topple her over so she closed her mind to it, closed her mind to everything aside from the need to enjoy herself and let tomorrow deal with the rest.

They staggered in a jerky embrace towards the kitchens, which they had been using for themselves since they had been holed up. They barely made it there. Her hands were scrabbling over him, raking along his spine and cupping his pulsing erection through the still damp swimming trunks. They kissed as they backed towards the kitchens, pushing open the door, which swung back behind them.

The privacy in the hotel was liberating, conducive to sex wherever they landed and whenever they wanted.

For the past few days they had greedily done whatever they had wanted because there had been no one to witness their stolen passion.

Grace felt herself butt against the edge of one of the cool granite work surfaces and gasped as he lifted her off her feet, settling her on the worktop.

She was wearing no more than a flimsy cotton dress and he shoved it up, urging her to wriggle so that he could push it underneath her. He parted her legs with his hands and Grace arched back, hands extended so that she was supporting herself. She was breathing fast, loosing tiny whimpering moans from her parted lips, eyes fluttering shut, holding the image of his dark head lowering with intent between her thighs.

He nuzzled her through her panties, breathing her in and teasing her with little darts from his tongue. He didn't bother taking them off. She could easily have shifted so that he could have pulled them down and done away with them altogether but, instead, he played with her until she was losing her mind with wanting more.

When he finally pulled the crotch of the panties to one side and inserted his tongue into her wetness, Grace was a heartbeat away from coming. She held on for as long as she could, but it was impossible to resist the insistent thrusting of his tongue as it found her sensitive clitoris and probed it with devastating effect.

Her orgasm was so powerful that she wobbled on the counter, almost falling backwards. She was relieved when he eased her off in one swift, effortless motion to deposit her on the long sofa, one of three that made the kitchen such a comfortable space. Groaning from the aftermath of coming, Grace was aware of Nico ridding himself of his swimming trunks and she barely had time to absorb his rampant erection, as hard as steel, when he thrust into her. One move, deep and hard and taking her beyond what she had experienced the first time. One move and he shuddered against her before collapsing to the side. It wasn't quite wide enough for the two of them and he was practically falling off, not that she really noticed because she was spent.

The dress was still on and he primly patted it back over her thighs.

'That's what happens,' Nico murmured, 'when a guy goes swimming and spends the whole time thinking about the woman waiting for him when he gets back to dry land. Think that's what sailors felt when they spent months at sea? Think that's why so many children were fathered when they returned from their trips back to hearth and home?'

'Sometimes,' Grace said drowsily, 'the fathering didn't necessarily include the hearth and home…'

'Very astute.' He chuckled and pushed her hair from her face so that he could plant a gentle kiss on her forehead.

It was so tender a gesture that her heart constricted.

For just a moment, she wondered whether this was what love felt like when it was returned. The gentle kiss after the explosive sex, the whispered words, the holding close. The planning for a shared future and the hopes and dreams waiting to materialise.

How could something so far from returned love mimic the real thing? How could life be so cruel? How could she have ended up where she had when she'd thought that all her defences were up and running?

How?

'Nico…' She sighed and twisted away. There was just the one window in the kitchen and the shutters were half closed. Through them she could just about glimpse snatches of darkness outside, could hear the rustle of night-time insects in the still, hot air.

The beaches looked different after the hurricane, with toppled trees yet to be cleared away and debris that had either been washed in from the turbulent seas or swept down from the battered land, but nothing could disguise the true blue of the water as it returned to its placid beauty or the icing-sugar softness of the sand drying out nicely under the steady sunshine.

Grace would never forget any of it. Not the sights or the sounds of this lazy tropical island. It was so different from anything she'd ever experienced. Nico was resting against her, idly stroking her breast through the dress, and she shifted a little. 'I'm thinking that the airstrip is back open for business and the work we began when we came here is finished…'

Nico stilled.

He was still on a high after some of the best sex

he'd ever had. He heard what sounded like a serious conversation in the making and for once, post sex, he wasn't interested. Accustomed to leaping out of bed the very second business between the sheets was concluded, he had discovered a liking here for staying put and winding down with a warm and willing body next to him. *This* warm and willing body next to him. The last thing he felt like was a dissection of deals that needed doing back in London.

When he had first slept with Grace, he had accepted, as a given, that whatever brief fling they had would disappear the second they touched down at Heathrow. The thought of sleeping with his secretary, once back to the cut and thrust of his high-octane city life, was frankly unacceptable.

He was a firm believer in several hundred lines of separation between work and his personal life. There was no way he could see anything but trouble on the horizon if he were to ever take another route.

And it was more than that. He knew the kind of woman he needed in his life when it came to commitment and Grace didn't fit the bill, however hot the sex was.

Out here, he was happy to go with the flow, but that wasn't his nature and it would never be the right path for him.

Now, as she threw that timely reminder into the mix, Nico asked himself why he was so reluctant to admit that she was right, that they couldn't stay here much longer.

Was it because he wasn't ready for this to end?

He hadn't anticipated that taboo sex could feel so good. Just lying here next to her made his erection begin to stir back into enthusiastic life.

Women had always been so predictable. Grace, though…in a heartbeat, things had changed between them. It felt as though bit by gradual bit he had peeled away layers of her and the more he peeled away, the more he sensed there was to discover.

Was it any wonder that he wasn't quite ready to relinquish the challenge of digging deeper?

Would it get complicated once they returned to work? Weren't there exceptions to every rule? Besides, if he lost control physically, he never would in any other area. That just wasn't the man he had conditioned himself to be.

He could think out of the box… Wouldn't he wean himself off this by carrying on? Wean them *both* off this…by not killing what they had prematurely?

Nico luxuriated in multiple scenarios in which what they had might carry on until such time as inevitable boredom seeped in.

Having never had to put himself out when it came to holding onto a woman, he surprised himself with the number of creative reasons he could now come up with to justify hanging onto what they had started.

The disgruntlement he had felt when she had broached the topic of their mission here coming to a close disappeared. He quietly congratulated himself on being able to see everything from all possible angles, thereby finding a solution to whatever thorny issue was at hand.

On this occasion, the thorny issue of them not having reached the natural conclusion to this affair.

'Don't talk,' he purred. Before she could protest, he was silencing her with a gentle finger over her lips. 'Let me do the talking.'

He leapt off the sofa, turned around and held out his hand, which Grace took, though she seemed reluctant. He pulled her to her feet and then to him, so that their bodies were pressed against one another, and he cupped her rear with his hands and gently massaged until she could feel the thoughts draining out of her head.

'Nico…'

'You raise a good point. We have to talk. And we will…just as soon as we have a nice, long shower and get dressed and come back down here to prepare something to eat. Don't forget, I've just swum the equivalent of the Channel crossing…'

'At the very least…'

He was already leading her out of the kitchen and she followed him without resistance. Nico, holding her hand, was brimming over with the exultation of having found a way to quieten his frustration at reality beckoning.

He idly glanced around him as they headed through the small boutique hotel up to the suite where they had taken up residence together.

Of course, he had become accustomed to these

surroundings. To start with, he had barely noticed them. He had arrived to do a job and doing the job hadn't included appreciation of what his uncle had done. In truth, he had been so prejudiced against Sander that he had come fully prepared to scorn everything his uncle had touched.

Nico didn't know how and when things had changed but, as Grace had mused on a couple of occasions, the hotel and everything that went with it, from the successful fishing business to the loyalty of all his employees, spoke of a guy who had landed on the island as a confused and washed-up man only to find purpose and direction and a reason for living.

Now, Nico thought that it might have been okay to have known this guy his uncle had become.

He would never have had time for the man who had wasted his youth and recklessly threatened the future of the family business but, yes, he would have had time for the man who had found his way.

Nico was vaguely aware that Grace wasn't her usual self. He felt that she wasn't a woman who lived in the moment. He felt that sleeping with him would have been her biggest break with caution. With London looming she would thinking ahead to them going their separate ways and if she felt the way he did, then she would be at war with herself, wanting more yet uneasily aware of the siren call of common sense. He knew her so well. Well enough to realise that she would never throw herself at him and plead for more, but she wouldn't have to. He would hold out his hand, she would take it and they would return to London and finish what they'd started.

He coaxed her in the wet room with expert hands that soaped her all over…and he murmured just the right words to have her smiling and then laughing as they headed back down to the kitchen, and when she hesitantly looked at him with a question in her eyes and something close to anxiety shadowing her delicate features, he distracted her by talking about Sander and the thoughts that had come to him as they had walked through the hotel earlier.

She was a good listener. She rarely interrupted and she never threw her opinions into the mix or else, if she did, then they were always opinions he was interested in hearing.

She *got* him and that was one of the reasons why he was so confident that when the time came they would remain…friends.

Beyond that…

He frowned, because there could never be anything beyond that. She had told him that her life had been normal. He'd never expected otherwise. For a few moments, he wondered what would happen if he didn't define what they had with timelines, if he gave it a chance, waited to see where it would lead. Almost as fast, he dismissed the notion. She would always deserve better than a man trained to put work ahead of everything else.

'You were saying,' Nico revived the conversation begun earlier, 'that things we came to do here have been done.' He watched as delicate colour crawled into her face although she didn't turn to meet his eyes.

He could read what was going through her head and he savoured the anticipation of dispelling all her unasked questions.

Filled with a sense of intense satisfaction, he stopped the chopping, dumped the knife on the counter and swivelled so that he was looking at her, hip against the counter, legs lightly crossed.

Grace stiffened, but eventually she couldn't kid herself that he wasn't staring at her.

Even though she'd known that this moment was going to come, she still felt unprepared. Things had to end, and she only wished that she had stood her ground and got in there with her speech first, before him.

Now she was going to be at the receiving end of one of his *Dear John* talks, and the only consolation was that she wouldn't be sending a bunch of flowers to herself.

At least she wouldn't be weeping and wailing and making a nuisance of herself, whatever she happened to be feeling inside. And at least she had not once given in to the temptation to over-confide. She'd respected his boundaries and kept her dignity and pride in place.

She wondered whether she could head him off at the pass, but when she finally met his eyes it was to find determination stamped there along with…

a suggestion of satisfaction. Or maybe it was *relief* that she had broached a subject that might have been playing on his mind.

She hadn't got the impression that he was fed up with her, but then he was a guy who knew how to keep his cards close to his chest when it suited him.

Grace felt her heart thud inside her. She wanted to look away, but she couldn't. She had become too used to feasting her eyes on him, appreciating his sheer masculine beauty. She guarded her love like a thief with stolen treasure but when it came to lust, there were no holds barred. He enjoyed her looking at him, devouring him greedily with her eyes, and she had always been more than happy to oblige.

'What we have here...' Nico paused but only for a couple of seconds. 'I don't want it to end.' He gestured and smiled at her ruefully and with some bewilderment. 'I know... I know...this isn't how I expected things to play out but something about you, Grace... I see you and I want to touch.' He shrugged his shoulders with yet more incomprehension.

Nico noted that she was staring at him with a dumbfounded expression and he smiled slowly,

'And you want it too,' he murmured with sweeping self-assurance. He reached out and placed his hand at the nape of her neck and absently stroked the sensitive skin while he continued to maintain the sort of eye contact that would have had most women reaching for the smelling salts. 'I touch you and you go up in flames. Like me. I don't understand it but

I'm not going to fight it. I know,' he continued with the same, mesmerising softness, 'you might have some concerns that if we continue with what we have, it might impact on our work relationship, but it won't. Trust me. I've never mixed business with pleasure but there's a first for everything and this is going to be my first…'

CHAPTER EIGHT

'*TRUST* YOU THAT it won't make a difference to our working relationship?'

Grace managed to get her vocal cords into working order, but she was still gaping at him with incredulity.

This wasn't what she had expected. She had expected to be gently given her walking papers. So he was now saying that he wanted things to carry on? That he didn't want things to end? Grace knew him so well that she could read everything between the lines, everything that hadn't been actually *said* but was there as big and as bold as a billboard advertisement.

Nico hadn't expected things to have ended up where they had. She doubted he'd ever looked at her twice until that fateful accident of chance when he'd bumped into her on her pointless Internet date. Maybe he'd seen her for the first time, then, as a woman rather than an extremely efficient robot? Maybe his curiosity had been piqued? He was never one to deny the beckoning of sexual curiosity—being marooned on an island that was the essence of heady romance might have prompted him into doing what he would never, ever have done within the confines of an office. As he'd just said, he'd never mixed business with pleasure.

At any rate, here they were and what he was essentially saying to her in that charming, self-deprecating, humbly confused way of his was that he wasn't ready for the sex to end *yet*.

That it would end was a given. It had always been a given. He was simply, now, laying down his terms for when it ended.

Grace knew that she should not be annoyed by that, and she definitely shouldn't be surprised because that was how his love life functioned. He called the shots.

The very thought of him shoving her into the same category as all the other women he had dated made her grit her teeth and clench her fists and want to throw something hard and heavy at his handsome head.

Did he honestly think that she was now so much under his magnetic spell that she would do as requested? Was their relationship now puppet master with the empowering hand and pliable, mindless puppet with no more self-determination?

Unfortunately, she could see just why he might have come to that conclusion, and she winced with bitter regret that she hadn't had the strength to walk away when she'd had the chance, but her own secret longings had been dry tinder to a match suddenly struck. She had gone up in flames because her fantasies had suddenly come true.

She surfaced to hear him in full flow, and she frowned. 'Sorry, I missed that...'

'For me there would be no problem working with you. Yes, yes, yes... I know what you're going to say. You're going to say that I was never a man who encouraged work and play to happen in the same place. You're going to remind me of those times when I've complained at calls interrupting meetings and unexpected visits screwing up my work schedule, but aren't there always exceptions to every rule? Isn't that a sign of flexibility? Not being tied down to dogma? It's no good lamenting the fact that we started this. In fact, I don't regret a minute of it.' He shot her a devilish smile. 'Would it be so wrong of me to say that I think we're on the same page with this? Making love has never felt so good. Just thinking of you gives me a hard-on and that's a first for me. So we're both adults and if we break new ground by seeing one another and working with one another as well, then who are we hurting?'

'So to recap,' Grace said slowly, 'what you're saying is that we carry on having this...fling when we return to London because we're both adults and why bother to try and find the energy and willpower to call it quits when we can just carry on going with the flow until...well, until the whole thing fizzles out.'

He'd announced his offer with a note of triumph and all guns blazing, assured of victory.

For him, she was just someone else, another body he wasn't quite tired of.

For her, he was the embodiment of everything she knew she shouldn't want or love but wanted and loved anyway.

The man beyond cynicism had met someone not cynical enough.

'How long do you think that'll take?'

'Who can put a number on something like that?'

'Actually, if I had to think of one person who could, then it would probably be you.'

'What do you mean?'

'Come on, Nico,' Grace said gruffly, 'if I had to keep a diary of how long your relationships last, then I'd say none of them go beyond the three-month watershed.'

'I'm sure you're wrong on that score.' But he was frowning and thinking. 'At any rate, this is different. What we have is nothing like what I've had in the past with…the other women I've dated, so it's impossible to go down the comparison road.'

'I'm guessing I should be flattered?'

'*I'm* flattered you looked twice at me,' he responded with sincerity. 'Seeing that you came from a standpoint of disapproval. Do you remember that conversation we had? When you opened up about my dating habits?'

Grace shivered. From that perfectly accurate assessment, it surely would only be a hop and a skip before he started coming to all sorts of conclusions, some of which might be right.

This time she was definitely going to head him away from the pass before that clever brain of his started joining dots.

'I remember.' She shrugged and smiled distantly. 'Maybe that's why we're in this place now. Neither of us saw it coming but it worked, *out here*, because we took what we wanted and had some fun.'

'Run that by me?'

'You enjoyed the novelty and so did I.'

'The novelty…'

'I mean, we worked alongside one another for a long time, and I guess, thrown together like this…' She glanced around her and left it up to him to interpret where she was going with what she had just said. 'Curiosity got the better of us. It happens. Doesn't mean it has to keep on happening! Realistically, I think we're both too sensible for that, don't you?'

He liked novelty but there was no reason why he had to have the monopoly on that.

She stepped back and slowly wiped her hands on one of the kitchen towels, then she retreated to the safety of a kitchen chair, swivelling it so that she was looking at him.

Her legs felt like jelly. She could tell from the shadow of sudden uncertainty in his eyes that the conversation wasn't going in the predicted direction.

All of this, the arrogant assumption that she would

fall in line…the glib acceptance that she would want to hang onto what he was offering because what woman wouldn't? She hated herself for still loving him because it defied everything sensible inside her.

However, Grace still possessed sufficient common sense to know just where this was going to go, and Nico Doukas was about to find out what it felt like to have the rug pulled from under his feet.

She intended to play by *her* rules, even though this was anything but a game.

'You don't mean that…do you? I can *feel* the desire coming off you in waves. It's telling me something else, another story…' He strolled towards her and then made her treacherous heart flutter like crazy when he leant over, propping himself on the arms of her chair and suffocating her with his unbearable proximity.

What would she do if he kissed her now?

Push him forcefully back? Turn away with freezing intent? Cave in and loop her arms around his neck and return that kiss?

'It's not going to happen, Nico.' This because option three felt dangerously tempting. She placed her hands on his chest, felt the heat of his body burning through the tee shirt and clenched her jaw. She didn't push but the intent was there and after a few seconds, during which she saw bewilderment register on his face, he drew back but remained in place in front of her, staring down with a frown.

'Oh, Grace, my darling…'

'I don't think it's tenable for this to continue after we leave here.'

My darling...if only she were...

'Why not?'

Grace shrugged. 'Because it just isn't.'

'Are you telling me that you've abruptly stopped being attracted to me? Maybe you're saying that once we land in London, the attraction will conveniently disappear...because if that's what you're saying, then we could always put it to the test.'

'Nico...this has been fun.'

Her voice was gentle. She was being reasonable. She was letting him down the way she imagined he was accustomed to letting down the women he inevitably got bored with. In her head she was thinking, *I still need this job, but tomorrow the search begins for a replacement, because I'll never really be able to share space with this man without hurting.*

'But we both know this is going nowhere and *you* might not have a problem carrying on with it until it fizzles out, but *I* have.'

'Why?' he questioned, eyes narrowing.

Grace could see him thinking, working things out, joining dots that she didn't want him to join.

'Because I want more for myself,' she told him quietly and truthfully. 'I'm thirty-one years old and I have no intention of wasting my time with something that's not going anywhere. We get along and the sex has been great fun but that's where it ends. Essentially, I'm not your type and you're not mine.'

Every word that passed her lips hurt but none of that hurt showed in her determined expression. 'And I'm not getting involved on a pointless joy ride that'll be over in the blink of an eye and whatever you say about it not affecting our working relationship, it probably would. There's a very good reason you say that you've never been tempted to mix business with pleasure and even if you're the boss and you can do exactly what you want, it's still not a good idea. How would it work? Practically?'

'What do you mean?' He flushed, and Grace's eyebrows shot up in an amused question.

'I mean, Nico, think about it. I get to the office usual time, bring you a cup of coffee, as per usual, and we spend the day…dovetailing around one another until the clock strikes six and then what? We lock the outside door and suddenly throw ourselves at one another and rip off our clothes and make wild love on your office desk?'

'Don't be ridiculous.'

'I'm not being ridiculous, Nico,' she said wryly. 'It would be embarrassing, and our working relationship would totally end up suffering.'

Not to mention her heart.

She thought of her mother, always searching for the right one, getting hurt along the way.

She had had little sympathy because of the fallout left in the wake of her mother's never-ending parade of possibilities. When her mother had disappeared to the other side of the world, Grace had resigned herself to it being the full stop to a chequered love life that had seen her have no time to spare for the children she had had.

Now, she had a reluctant admiration for the way Cecily had always picked herself up, dusted herself down and carried on. She hadn't been the most responsible parent on the planet, but all those knocks along the way would have hurt and yet she had still played her acting games with Grace and her brother, like the kid she essentially had been, and dazzled her way through her hurt. And Australia? Perhaps that had finally been True Love. Who was Grace to begrudge her that? She had disappeared leaving her adult children behind to look out for themselves and maybe that was just tough love. Maybe that had been all she had had to give.

Loving Nico had opened Grace's horizons and shown her the nuances in life. It was seldom a case of black and white, with the right guy coming along, ticking all the boxes with no broken hearts along the way because measures had been put in place to protect those hearts. She had been so careful, had assured herself that she had learnt all the lessons necessary to make sure she controlled her love life instead of her love life controlling her, and yet, here she was, ambushed by the very thing she had fought to protect herself from.

At least her pride hadn't been flushed down the drain. At least she had only allowed Nico to see sides to her that she wanted him to see.

How many times, in those lazy moments when they had been flushed and content after making love, had she been tempted to tell him about her childhood? About the stress of having Cecily for a mother? The responsibilities that had been shouldered when she'd been just a kid? About Tommy and all the problems now on her plate?

She had held back because a little voice inside had warned her that oversharing would be a mistake.

Whatever her feelings for Nico, he would never have appreciated that level of depth because, in his eyes, what they had had just been a bit of fun. Exciting and thrilling but just some fun.

Now, she was glad that she had held back because she would carry on working for him until she got another job and she would pretend that everything was fine. She would do what her mother had been an expert at doing. She would put a smile on her face and dust herself off and carry on.

She had to smile when she thought how much she had fought against having anything in common with Cecily. Now, she sincerely hoped her acting skills were up to scratch.

'Of course, I'm very flattered.' Grace offered a placating smile. 'But like I've said, you know that I'm a sensible person...'

'I never thought I'd hate the sound of someone being sensible,' Nico growled.

Grace overrode the interruption. 'I'm sensible enough to know that whatever dying embers of attraction might still be there when we get back to London, it would be sheer folly to fan them into life.'

'That's a very overblown way of saying that the sex is great. So why stop when the going's good? Anyone would think that this is about more than what's on the table.'

'What do you mean?'

'I mean this is great sex. It's not a *Gone with the Wind* searing love story.'

'I know *that*.' She laughed dismissively. 'Do you honestly think I'd be crazy enough to read more into this than what's there?' She raised her eyebrows and rolled her eyes and made a convincing show of indifference mixed with amusement. 'Like I said, Nico, let's put this behind us when we get to London. We have a lot to do…deals that have been hanging in the balance…'

Nico looked at her narrowly for a few seconds, then he shrugged and threw her a shadow of a smile.

He raised both hands in a gesture of rueful resignation.

'You can't blame a guy for trying.'

They were back on track. Grace should have been relieved, but she felt a punch of misery at what was being lost.

'Shall we carry on with our evening? Seeing as it'll probably be the last?' She kept smiling and chatting as she busied herself adding the final touches to their meal. She wanted him to keep asking and yet she knew that her answer would be the same how-

ever much he asked. She felt his dark eyes on her and
her body tingled and burned, but when she finally
turned to look at him, she was still smiling and there
was nothing there to give her pain away.

Nico was sitting at his desk three days later, frustrated with himself because things couldn't have
been more normal between them and yet the normality, which he should have welcomed, felt like
a shard of glass that wouldn't leave him alone. He
looked at her down-bent head as she did what she
always did, made notes on her iPad of things to do,
and he pictured her naked beneath him...on top of
him...looking at him over her shoulder...her cool
eyes turning him on in ways he'd never been turned
on in his life before.

When she wasn't in his presence, he thought of
her. He couldn't concentrate. Images of her kept sur-
facing, interrupting him when he was desperate to
focus. It got on his nerves.

Was this preoccupation of his to do with the fact
that she had been the one to end things?

Surely he couldn't be *that* shallow? *That* self-cen-
tred?

They hadn't slept together after she'd told him
to get lost. On the surface, they'd reverted to what
they had been before, two people with a successful
working relationship. The boss and his secretary.
Gradually, conversation had returned to work and
the passion they'd shared had been papered over.

By the time they'd touched down in London, it had felt as though the intimacy that had been so real had vanished like dew in the summer sun.

He swivelled his chair to stare through the window and was frowning and gazing out when he heard her clear her throat.

'Am I interrupting?'

Nico swung the chair round, pushed it back and resisted the urge to scowl. Instead, he bared his teeth in something resembling a smile. A ferocious, slightly terrifying smile.

Naturally the frothy summer clothes had gone. She was back to the serious stuff. Today was a pale grey knee-length skirt and a white cotton top and a cardigan, which she had yet to remove even though it was mid-afternoon and the office was warm.

He *still* wanted to touch her. He *still* had an insane urge to rip off the prim and proper layers and get to her nakedness, feel her bare body, her nipples, the dip of her belly button. He *still* wanted to hear her whimper as he got between her legs and teased her with his tongue.

He emphatically *didn't* want to hear her ask him about some legality on some merger of some company.

'Not at all,' he drawled, vaulting upright and moving towards the pale leather sofa where his jacket had been tossed earlier in the day. 'It's Friday. It's been a roller coaster couple of weeks. I suggest we both knock off early.'

He paused and wondered whether she would pick up on the ambiguity, but she tilted her head to one side, tucked her hair behind her ears and smiled politely.

'Have you got exciting plans for this evening? For the weekend?'

'Not at the moment. But I intend to.' He slung on the jacket and thought, with a distinct lack of enthusiasm, that he could have plans if he chose to pick up the phone to any number of women he knew would happily go out with him wherever he chose to take them.

Hell, why shouldn't he?

And why shouldn't she know what his plans were?

Hadn't they returned to their previous working relationship? The one where she knew him like the back of her hand? The one where she knew what all his plans were because she arranged them on his behalf?

'See if you can get me a table for two tomorrow at that little French restaurant I like in Pimlico, would you?' He didn't look at her. He looked at his phone, began scrolling through it.

'French restaurant?'

'You know the one. Candles and vases of flowers on the tables and waiters with French accents pretending they don't understand a word of English.'

Grace knew the one.

Of course, he wouldn't have waited long before he picked up where he'd left off with his fan club.

He was a guy who moved on. She knew that but it didn't help. Every pore and fibre in her body hurt with a pain that was indescribable. She smiled with frozen politeness and nodded.

'What time?'

'Hmm…' He glanced at his Rolex. 'Eight sounds about right. We can loosen up with a drink at the pub opposite before.' He dealt her a slashing smile. She returned with a brilliant, thousand-wattage one of her own.

'And you? Hectic weekend fun?'

Grace hesitated.

She would be seeing Tommy the following evening.

She'd phoned him as soon as she'd got back but he had seemed less enthused to hear from her than she'd expected and she'd wondered what was wrong.

In a flash, all the worries she had blithely cast aside during her heady stay on the island had returned in full force. He could be moody. She didn't blame him because he had suffered so many setbacks for someone as young as he was and he just didn't have the stamina to deal with them.

She had asked him to come to her place instead of her going to his as she usually did.

The change of scenery might do him a power of good. He would stay over and she would pamper him and listen to him and get him back on track.

She surfaced to find Nico staring at her intently

and she wondered whether he was making assumptions that her weekend would be an uneventful one. Their eyes met and she shifted and flushed and then said, a little defiantly, 'I have plans, as a matter of fact.' *Completely true,* she thought wryly, although *adventurous* would be a definite overstatement.

'Really? Going anywhere exciting?'

'The excitement will be at my place,' she chirped. 'I plan on cooking a really fantastic meal...'

'Special occasion?'

Grace blushed and shrugged mysteriously and looked away all at the same time and when she spoke it was to throw over her shoulder that she would text and email him confirmation of his dinner booking.

He was still standing, hands shoved into his trouser pockets, a slight frown on his face, but then his expression cleared, returned to one of lazy amusement and he nodded and began galvanising himself back into action.

'Walk down with me,' he murmured, pausing as she bustled out to her desk and began busying herself with her computer.

'I...' Grace glanced at him, heart pounding, desperate to get out of his presence so that she could wallow in her misery that he had resumed his old life without so much as a backward nod to what they had shared. For a few breathless seconds, their eyes locked and it felt as though the air between them had been drained of oxygen. She knew, with dismay, that her cheeks were on fire when she at last managed to break eye contact. 'I…have one or two things to do before I leave, Nico.'

'What?'

'Some emails to get through…that report with the financial figures still has to be compiled for Robert in Accounts…'

Nico sauntered towards her and gently but firmly pressed shut her computer with one autocratic finger.

'No, you don't. I'm the boss and I'm giving you permission to stop work for the day.'

'And also to walk down with you? Is that an order as well?' She'd been aiming for light, but she heard a sarcastic, resentful edge to her voice that he picked up on because his expression cooled.

'Is this where we are, Grace? You'll only actually walk ten steps with me out of this office if I tell you that you have to?'

'No, of course not!' Hot colour stained her cheeks and she licked her lips, mortified because he was right. This wasn't where she wanted to be. Yet how could it ever be possible to feel normal around him when she was in love with him? When they had been lovers?

She gathered her things at speed, conscious of his eyes on her as he waited.

'What will everyone think?' This to try and lighten the sudden tension between them, but her voice was brittle and her smile was watery. Inadvertently, she had alluded to the relationship they had shared and she went even redder. 'I mean…' she stammered, then fell into awkward silence.

'What *will* everyone think?' Nico purred silkily. 'By everyone, I take it you're referring to everyone we're going to pass on the way to the elevator?'

'This isn't funny, Nico.'

'You're my secretary,' he said mildly. 'I think it's safe to say that no one is going to think anything. Are you afraid your reputation might be ruined?' His eyebrows shot up and he stepped back to open the outer door so that she could precede him. He leant to whisper in her ear. 'Only you and I know the truth, don't we, Grace?' He pulled back and briskly walked away and she hurried after him. 'Your reputation is already so interestingly sullied…'

If the merest mention of *anything* to do with what they'd had opened a Pandora's box, then it was obvious that she was going to have to be very careful to skirt round it all and truly pretend none of it had happened. Her ears were burning and her throat was dry at the flurry of images those wickedly whispered words provoked. It reminded her that her hunt for another job would have to be an urgent one because how much more would it take for her to just be able to control her wayward responses?

He was off on his hot date!

Yet, he wasn't averse to alluding to their brief affair. Did he think it was funny to embarrass her?

She was hot all over as they rode the elevator down

to the basement and she looked at him with alarm as
it shuddered to a stop.

'Where are we?'

'I'll give you a lift home.'

'No!'

'Why not?' The doors slid open and he stood to
one side, which compelled her to slip past him although she immediately turned around, her hands
on her hips.

'Because…because…'

'Are you scared?'

'Scared?' Her voice was pitched a few decibels
higher. 'Scared of what?'

'Scared of this,' Nico muttered, sotto voce.

And just like that, before she could do anything,
before she could pull back or turn away or even get
her thoughts in order, he was leaning into her. He
held her, a gentle enough hold but powerful enough
to stay her and his mouth covered hers.

His kiss was hungry, his tongue probing as it
moved against hers, caressing and greedy and *wanting* all at the same time.

Time stood still. Wetness pooled between her legs
and muscle memory made her lean towards him, devouring him just as he was devouring her.

She wanted this to stop immediately and she
wanted it to go on and on and on for ever.

Disobedient hands strayed upwards to wind
around his neck and the heat of his hard body against
hers filled her with giddy, guilty pleasure. His fin-

gers lightly threaded a blistering path along her collarbone and her breath hitched in her throat and her eyelids fluttered. Oh, how she could remember the way he had made her body feel!

She heard the clacking of footsteps echoing in the cavernous underground car park and yanked back, half stumbling in the process and automatically tugging her clothes into some kind of order.

Sanity was like a bucket of cold water, drowning her with shame and mocking her for her weakness. She jerked back and stared at him with wide, horrified eyes.

'How *dare* you?'

'How dare I *what*?'

Nico raked his fingers through his hair and looked away. He was furious with himself. Furious with himself for not being able to get her out of his system…for wanting to touch when he'd been knocked back…for not being able to resist temptation when it had been put in front of him. Everything about what had just happened exemplified the sort of weakness he had trained himself to despise.

God, even now, as his dark eyes rested on her swollen lips, he had to fight against moving towards her even if only to breathe her in.

Being on that island had perhaps put the misdeeds of his uncle into some kind of perspective but there was no way he had any time for emotions ruling his head, whatever change of perspective he might have had. Never had, never would.

The frustration right now was intense.

'You have my apologies,' Nico muttered in a driven undertone.

Tension was tearing through her body as she stared at him, her mouth still bruised from his, her body still wanting more, still burning for him.

He'd apologised but there had been no need because there was nothing for him to apologise about. She'd kissed him back as hungrily as he'd kissed her. She'd wanted him with every fibre of her being.

The only difference was he'd kissed her, she knew, to prove a point. To prove that she was still turned on by him. She, however, had kissed *him* because she'd had no choice. Her body had not been able to obey what her head had been saying.

He was moving on where she was standing still, and she would carry on standing still just so long as she was in his presence.

Grace took a deep, steadying breath.

'This isn't going to work,' she said quietly.

'You have my word that nothing of the kind will ever happen again,' Nico said heavily. 'God knows what I was thinking.'

'You wanted to prove to me that you could still… have an effect on me.' She supplied the answer before he could fill in the blanks himself. 'I expect…

you must find it all very amusing, that someone of my age could be as—'

'Don't say it, Grace,' he interrupted thickly. 'I could never be that person.'

'I might still find you attractive, Nico,' Grace said, gathering all her pride, 'but that doesn't mean that it's any more annoying than that.'

'Annoying…'

'What else? It's an inconvenient attraction. Nothing more.'

'Of course,' he said stiffly.

'But it's there and it's going to be impossible for us to continue working together. I thought…it might not intrude but…'

'My fault.'

'No one's fault, Nico. It is what it is. Tomorrow I'll begin looking for another job.'

The pain that tore into her as she uttered those words made her feel dizzy and sick. That she had actually already begun the exercise made no difference. She had openly stated her intention and now it was written in stone, a declaration of intent from which she could not, now, withdraw.

'No need.'

'What do you mean?'

'The last thing I would want is for you to…feel uncomfortable at the office. We work far too closely together for that to be a bearable situation. Not that that's the point. I…you deserve better than to feel apprehensive whenever I'm around and I get it that you might, even though you have my word that what happened just then…an aberration…' Nico breathed out heavily, unable to meet her eyes and making sure to step back, to put distance between them. 'You can leave without working your notice.'

'I beg your pardon?'

Nico smiled crookedly. 'This isn't how I ever saw our…working relationship playing out, but you've been the best… I wouldn't even call you my secretary because you've been a hell of a lot more than that. My right-hand…woman. And, Grace…' he pressed his thumbs against his eyes and then looked at her steadily '… I… I'll miss you, but you would be more comfortable not having to come in, so don't. As of this moment, I'm relieving you of your duties. You'll be paid for as long as it takes for you to find another job and I guarantee that I will give you the most glowing reference you could hope to get.'

'You mean…'

'I mean you can return to the office, clear your desk and say farewell to this building with no obligations to ever set foot in it again.'

'But what about my replacement?'

'I'll manage, Grace.' He tipped his hand in a mocking salute. 'I'm a big boy now.'

CHAPTER NINE

NICO LOOKED AT the woman sitting across from him at the table in the romantic restaurant that Grace had somehow found the time to book between clearing her desk and leaving copious notes for whoever happened to replace her.

How had she managed that?

Nico had no idea. She must have worked until midnight. At any rate, he had returned to the office early this morning and it was as if the woman who had been by his side for so many years, the oil that lubricated the engine of his working life, had never been.

The desk had been empty. The two plants had gone. The work computer had been sitting squarely in the middle of the empty desk and the stack of neatly typed notes had told its own story of dedication to the last.

Nico surfaced to the sound of silence and his blonde date staring at him with gimlet-eyed disapproval.

'I thought this evening was going to be fun.' She pouted, toying with the stem of her wine glass.

'So did I,' Nico concurred.

She was everything any red-blooded man could want in a date when it came to looks. Long blonde hair, falling like a sheet over narrow tanned shoulders. Big, baby-blue eyes and breasts that refused to be constrained by the strappy top she was wearing. She was an easily recognised catwalk model and every head had swung round the second they had entered the restaurant.

Unfortunately for Nico, as soon as he had seen her emerging from the chauffeur-driven Bentley he had sent to collect her, he had realised that the last thing he'd wanted was a date with Flavia Destyn. Politeness had prevented him from doing what he had wanted to do and making up a something and nothing excuse to back out but now…having spent the past forty-five minutes in stony silence while his mind whirred with images of Grace, he could no longer pretend that he wasn't bored out of his wits.

And it wasn't Flavia's fault.

'I have a lot on my mind at the moment,' he continued truthfully. He sat back as the exquisite fish dish he couldn't remember ordering was placed in front of him, but he continued to look at his date, aware that he had already concluded that the evening wasn't going to be going anywhere that involved the two of them in the same space.

What was she doing?

Who was she seeing?

Had she gone back on the Internet in the space of a handful of days?

Was she meeting some hunk in her house and cooking him dinner?

He stabbed the fish and scowled.

'I know a very good way of taking your mind off whatever's bothering you,' Flavia cooed, reaching out and covering his hand with hers and turning her baby blues on him with smoky, sultry invitation.

'So do I,' Nico murmured, sliding his plate to one side and feeling a sense of purpose for the first time since he'd magnanimously dispatched his secretary from his life.

He watched the blonde preen coquettishly with triumph and felt a little bad because she was in for a rude awakening.

'You're a nice girl, Flavia, and I'm sure that under other circumstances it would have been nice to get to know you…more intimately…'

But my days of getting to know you or anyone else intimately are at an end because the only woman I'm interested in knowing intimately is doing God only knows what right now with someone else.

Sudden panic swept through Nico. He'd never thought himself a fanciful person but suddenly he was bombarded by very graphic and very unwelcome images of Grace in the arms of another man.

She wouldn't be.

She wasn't like that.

He knew her. He knew her as well as he'd known anyone in his life before, as well as he knew himself.

Maybe she was doing right now just what he was doing. Seeing someone because she needed distracting from an attraction that wasn't going anywhere. Inconvenient it might be, but that didn't mean it wasn't urgent and demanding, an attraction that no one else could erase.

And maybe that attraction was more than just annoying. Could it be that she felt the same way he did? Under that controlled exterior, was she hiding feelings for him? Because wasn't that what *he* had been doing? Hiding feelings he hadn't expected? Pretending that what he felt was something he could control? Something that hadn't got to the very core of him until it was so embedded that life without those feelings was unthinkable?

He had been so sure that he could plan the outcome of his life that he had had no defences in place to prevent the slow intrusion of a woman who had gradually become indispensable.

He had slept with her and not for a moment had he paid heed to the dangers right in front of him. The klaxons and alarm bells had been shrieking and yet he had gaily sallied forth, utterly oblivious.

Why would he have paid them a scrap of attention?

In his well-ordered world, Nico had set himself the goal of marrying for convenience.

Once, he had tried his luck elsewhere. Once,

he had opened the door to a gloriously impulsive woman who'd wanted everything. He had looked at his father's arranged marriage and figured he could do things differently. He'd fallen for a woman who had demanded more than he could give. What had started with the heat and urgency of courtship had crashed and burned in a welter of accusation and anger. She'd needed him there by her side twenty-four-seven. She'd wanted one hundred per cent attention and had complained bitterly when work demands had called him away. He'd tried, but his father's mantra about the importance of responsibility had come back to haunt him. If that was love, then love wasn't for him.

After nine months, he had retreated from the fray and accepted that the lessons he had grown up with had been right all along.

Love and emotions were chaos, and he just wasn't built to deal with chaos.

Chaos had been his uncle. Order had been his father. Experience had taught him that it was pointless to look for the middle road.

Nico had locked his heart away and thrown out the key.

He might enjoy life to the full, but he would never be a fool. He would always be in control of his responses and no one would ever cross the lines he had laid down. He might be less constrained than his father, who had married the right woman when he had been very young and had never strayed from the straight and narrow, but he would never be his uncle.

Nico had quietly believed himself immune to surprises when it came to matters of the heart.

Was it any wonder he had glibly glazed over at all the warning signs that had been posted along the way until he was here now with a growing sense of panic inside him that he might have left things too late?

He focused. Flavia's expression was changing from self-satisfied triumph to growing alarm. Very shortly the alarm would tip over into fury and Nico didn't think he had it in him to face the wrath of a rejected date.

'I should go,' he said quietly. He scrunched the linen napkin on the table and signalled to the waiter without taking his eyes off Flavia. 'My apologies for leaving, Flavia. This isn't your fault. I should not have contacted you.'

'You can't just *walk off* and leave me sitting here,' the blonde hissed, glancing around her at the well-manicured, expensive clientele. 'What are people going to think?'

'That I'm a bastard and a blind one at that for walking out on a beautiful woman.' Nico paused and glanced at his watch. Time was suddenly of the essence. His imagination was fired up with all kinds of scenarios and he didn't like any of them. 'You like Destra?' He named an exclusive club of which he was a member and she nodded, although the pout was still in place. 'You can gather up your friends and go there. Ask for Ronnie and tell him you and your friends are to be treated like royalty. Champagne and caviar until midnight.'

'But when will I see you again?'

'I wouldn't bank on any more dates in the future.' Nico began rising to his feet, asking her whether she wanted to accept his champagne compensation offer and then telling her that he would phone Ronnie in advance so that there were no problems at the door.

He vaguely registered that it was a result that his date hadn't thrown her dinner plate at him. Flavia might be a catwalk model and tough as nails when it came to guys, but walking out on her halfway through a meal was not something he would ever have considered doing, however bored he might have been with the conversation.

In this instance, though…?

He could have contacted his driver but this felt like a very personal mission so he detoured only to grab his Ferrari and, on the way, the most expensive bunch of flowers he could find that late in the evening from a florist's close to the Underground.

His body was alive with edgy restlessness, but he was doing something. He was figuring out his life and he was doing something about it. He only hoped it wasn't too late.

Tommy was talking. He seemed to have been talking for most of the dinner she had painstakingly prepared to the point where most of it was still on his plate.

Grace knew that she should be happy, but she felt as though she were being battered from all sides, which meant that most of the food on *her* plate also remained uneaten.

She'd been on a low when her brother had arrived that morning. She'd plastered a bright smile on her face, but her head had been worrying over the misery sitting like a lump in the pit of her stomach.

No more Nico. No more job. No more *anything*. Fair as he was, he had allowed her to walk away without the discomfort of having to work her notice.

She would have her pay kept intact for as long as it took for her to find suitable employment. His references would be glowing. Could she have asked for more? Hadn't she already concluded that working with him was going to be impossible?

And that kiss...

The nail in the coffin. So much had been given away in her response, in the way she had clung to him with the desperation of a drowning swimmer clutching at a lifebelt thrown in the water. He had seen and smelled and *tasted* all the passion that was still there, simmering under the surface, waiting to be ignited at the spark of a flame.

Good heavens, she had been asked to book a dinner date for him with his latest blonde, and, even knowing that he was back to his old tricks, she *still* hadn't been able to resist his touch. He had lazily and idly tried it on, and instead of pushing him away she had capitulated without even the whiff of a fight.

So now she was staring at a bottomless void and on top of that… Tommy.

She'd expected him to be querulous…in need of the usual soothing pep talk… She'd braced herself to bite down on any hint of impatience. Instead, he had been fighting fit and, having had a break from her, had decided that the time was right for him to launch into what, she assumed, had been on his mind for a while.

He wanted her to back off.

She was too intrusive. He felt stifled. He could manage just fine without her calling him all the time to make sure he hadn't done anything silly. He *knew* she meant well…he *knew* how bad things had been after the accident. But that was years ago, and it was time for her to do her own thing and stop fussing over him.

Then he had gentled his tone and informed her that he had met someone, a girl in the same block as him. They'd been seeing one another for nearly four months and he hadn't mentioned it because he knew that if he had she, Grace, would have given him so many well-intentioned warnings that she would have ruined the whole thing.

Now, as she stared at her beautiful and in her head permanently dependent kid brother, she had to struggle not to feel mortally wounded by everything he had just laid at her door.

He'd finally dived into the chicken pie she had cooked but she shoved her plate to one side.

When, she thought miserably, had she morphed from the sister who picked up the pieces to the sister who became a bore? She felt rejected in her love life, with all her silly expectations, and rejected by her own family, who clearly no longer needed her suffocating concern.

Tears pricked the backs of her eyes, but she squeezed the hand that suddenly covered hers.

'You're amazing, sis,' Tommy told her, his blue eyes caring. 'But it's time you let me live my life and you go and live yours. I feel you've always put your life on hold to look after Ma and then me and, okay, I've been pretty pathetic for a while, but I really thought about stuff when you were stuck out there and it's time for me to stand on my own two feet. Hey! You should be married with a kid of your own by now!'

Grace was struggling not to burst into tears of self-pity at that well-meaning but, oh, so way-off-target remark when the doorbell buzzed.

She wasn't expecting anyone, but she was glad for the distraction anyway.

How much more could she take? She was hopelessly in love with the wrong guy. Married with a kid of her own? She might as well try and find some magic red shoes and float her way to another planet because that was how impossible the dream of marriage and kids felt right now.

'Sorry to interrupt, Tommy. Doorbell!'

She fled, leaving Tommy to his chicken pie, and pulled open the door without thinking.

It took Grace a few seconds to register who was standing outside.

She saw the whole first—tall…male…impossibly handsome…

She noted the clothes—expensive…casual…dark trousers and a perfectly tailored designer polo…

She saw the flowers…well, in truth she'd seen better…

Then her brain tallied all those impressions and she flew back, eyes wide.

'What are *you* doing here?' Automatically Grace barred entry to the house by standing in front of the door, blocking him from sweeping past her.

'I've come…look, here. I got these for you.' Nico thrust the flowers at her and in response Grace looked at him coldly and folded her arms.

So…had he realised, after his bountiful gesture that she could leave without working her notice, that having an empty space with no one efficiently handling so much of his workload was going to be a bit harder than anticipated? Had he met his blonde bombshell and retrospectively realised that he would have to make his personal arrangements himself because it would take time to train up her replacement in the finer art of booking expensive, atmospheric restaurants? Not to mention sourcing just the right goodbye token when the time came. Come to think of it, why wasn't he clinking champagne glasses over a candlelit dinner with the bombshell, looking forward to a night of fun between the sheets? Never mind. Not her business. What *was* her business was the fact that he was planted in front of her door and she didn't want him there.

Had he shown up with a bunch of less than average flowers in the hope of wooing her back behind her desk?

Grace shuddered at the very thought.

'Shouldn't you be at an expensive French restaurant with your latest conquest?' she couldn't resist asking and he flushed.

'Will you let me in?'

'No.'

'Because you're busy entertaining *your* latest conquest?' Nico asked, his mouth twisting cynically, although his hot, brooding eyes were saying something she wasn't sure she quite understood.

'Who I'm with is none of your business, Nico.' She looked at the flowers and was filled with sudden rage. 'And if you think you can renege on your promise and get me back into the office to do my time because you've realised you can't cope with the hassle of finding somebody else, then forget it. And the flowers? Not up to scratch, Nico. If you'd told me in advance, I would have ordered a much more expensive bunch for myself to plead your case. Although my answer would have been exactly the same!'

Nico edged closer and Grace, in turn, feeling the heat from him and the stirrings of her own treacherous body, toughened her stance, stood straighter, her back ramrod straight.

'Grace...'

About to tell him that he needed to go, Grace was interrupted before she could open her mouth by Tommy calling her, asking who was at the door, his voice high and cheerful and then the sound of his slow steps heading towards the front door to join her.

She glanced over her shoulder and there he was, pausing to stand in the small hall, his head tilted to one side. So blond, so angelic and so...*so present at exactly the wrong time.*

'Tommy, please, could you go and wait for me in the...er...kitchen? I'll be with you in a sec.'

'Tommy?' Nico shifted closer to peer over her shoulder.

'Who's that?' Tommy flagrantly ignored Grace's request and padded over so that he was standing directly behind her. She could feel his warm breath on the back of her neck although her eyes were riveted by Nico and the dark, disapproving flush spreading across his handsome face.

'Please, Tommy...' She half turned to her brother, who was grinning at her, eyebrows raised. He looked as though he might launch into a conversation she didn't want.

'Tommy? Pleased to meet you.'

Grace was aghast as Nico reached past her, brushing her arm, to encourage her brother towards him, and she half closed her eyes when they shook hands, which proved awkward considering she had remained standing between them.

Her heart was hammering inside her like a sledgehammer. Her secrecy about her private life now made her burn with discomfort. She had kept her private life to herself as a self-defence mechanism! And what a good idea that had been, all things considered! But now it felt sly and overblown. Now, she wished she had confided in him. He would have listened. He would have given her sensible advice. He would have told her what Tommy had just told her…that she needed to stop playing full-time carer. He would have braced her for something that had come as a complete shock.

She wished she'd shared. She'd given him everything anyway, everything that really mattered. What had been the point in holding back the little details?

Nico, shifting awkwardly to inspect his competition, noted the guilty pinkening of Grace's cheeks.

Tommy?

Since when was she someone who abbreviated other people's names? Everyone else called James, the sales manager, Jimmy, and it had always amused him that she had never used that abbreviation. In fact, thinking about it, hadn't she once told him in that sexy, prim, husky voice of hers that she didn't have time for the annoying tendency people had to shorten anything and everything?

So… *Tommy*?

Nico felt something he had never felt in his life before and it ripped through him like shards of glass, cutting, wounding, making him bleed inside.

Jealousy.

It was an emotion he had never had time for, but it was very real now, and he felt his jaw ache as he clenched it in something he hoped was a passably indifferent smile.

So she had a guy over. So she had cooked him dinner. That didn't mean she'd moved on from *him*, did it?

He found that he was clutching the flowers so tightly that the stems were breaking and he hurriedly thrust the bunch at her, which took her somewhat by surprise.

'I haven't brought these because I'm trying to woo you back to the workplace,' he muttered.

His mind was occupied with the fair-haired guy who was still looking at him with open curiosity.

He looked like a kid. Fresh faced despite a certain seriousness lurking beneath the surface, something shadowed and disillusioned that spoke of life more eventful than would appear superficially. He wasn't a kid. He was a man with a backstory. He was a three-dimensional guy standing in the doorway of a woman he realised he'd always thought of as *his*. Jealousy tightened its grip.

'I suppose you'd better come in and tell me why you're here.' Grace stood aside reluctantly, shooing Tommy back into the kitchen, relieved when he did as she signalled although she made sure to funnel Nico away from the kitchen into the sitting room. She stood back and watched as he swung round to look at her for a few tense seconds.

'You moved fast.'

'I beg your pardon?'

'Who is he?'

'Nico, what are you talking about?' She narrowed her eyes and folded her arms.

He dominated the small sitting room, standing there, towering over her, his aggressive masculinity threatening every part of her and making her feel unprotected.

'The man,' Nico grated. 'New Internet sensation?'

'For heaven's sake!' Grace looked at him narrowly. 'Are you...*jealous*?'

I should have told you... I shouldn't have been so buttoned up.

'Jealous? I've never been jealous in my life before!'

Nico raked his fingers through his hair and stared at her before swinging away to drop into one of the chairs. He immediately leaned forward, hands on his thighs.

'I think I need a drink.'

Grace hesitated.

Of course, the last thing she wanted or *needed* right now was this man in her house, sending her already frazzled nervous system into yet more freefall.

And she certainly didn't need to feel this *guilt* about drawing the lines she had drawn.

He made her feel *alive* but was feeling *alive* a good thing? Hadn't it been so much easier to live life on one level? Not too high, not too low? The excitement flooding through her made her want to cry because it was a rushing tide she couldn't hold back.

'You need to tell me why you're here, Nico,' she finally managed to say.

'Okay. You're right. I'm… I suppose you could say…' he looked at her with smouldering accusation in his deep, ink-black eyes '…that I'm jealous.'

'You're *jealous*?' Grace quietly shut the sitting-room door behind her. If she knew Tommy, he would finish his chicken pie and reach for his mobile and probably, given what she now knew, immediately get in touch with his girlfriend for an hour-long conversation.

She sidled towards one of the chairs and then perched on it. Her tummy was full of butterflies. She had no idea where this was going but there was no way she could walk away from this edge-of-the-seat thrill sensation swirling inside her.

She linked her fingers and leant towards him.

'You asked me what I was doing here and whether I shouldn't be at that restaurant with a woman and the answer is yes. That's where I should be. That's where I was up until an hour ago but I found that it wasn't where I actually wanted to be.' He shook his head as though clearing it and continued, voice low, 'I couldn't get you out of my head, Grace. Where I wanted to be was with *you*. I came here because

I had no choice. I thought about you…and another man and it drove me nuts.'

Listening to Nico, hearing the ragged sincerity in his voice and seeing the urgency in his dark gaze, Grace felt her heart swell but with that came a warning voice of caution.

This wasn't love.

This was attraction. This was lust. He didn't want her back in the office. He wanted her back in his bed and he had come here because he had thought she was entertaining some guy.

The fact that he was jealous…well, Grace had to admit that that did something to her, sent little shivers racing up and down her spine. As did the way his eyes were burning into her.

Little did he know that he had nothing to be jealous about. She breathed in deeply.

'You have nothing to be jealous about.'

'I don't?' Long, lush lashes dropped to conceal his expression but there was a glitter in his eyes when he next looked at her.

'Tommy is…my brother.'

Afterwards, Grace would try and recapture in her head the sequence of expressions that flitted across Nico's face at that revelation but overwhelmingly it was one of utter stupefaction.

His mouth dropped open and for a few seconds he looked as though that sharp mind of his had been completely emptied.

'Sorry?'

'Tommy's my brother.'

'But you haven't got a brother.'

'What do you mean?'

'We… I thought…we shared…you would have told me if you had a brother.'

Nico felt that unexpected revelation like the force of a runaway train barrelling into him at full speed. It knocked him for six.

A brother?

He'd thought he knew her. Thought he knew her as well as she knew him. He'd shared more with her than he ever had with anyone in his life before. When he thought back to their time together on the island, before, even, he could see a trail of confidences left behind him. Barely acknowledged, just slipped into conversation in passing. He'd told her things he'd never told anyone. And yet, it had not been returned. No like for like.

It felt like treachery and it hurt.

Grace's throat constricted. How could she explain that talking about her childhood had felt dangerous? How could she tell him that she'd been so scared of turning him off her that she'd edited herself to be the person she'd thought he wanted? Someone who was in it just for the fun? That she'd held her private life close to herself because, in her head, she could envision him running a mile if she shared things that overstepped the boundaries between them?

How could she explain that she had made a mistake? In a rush, she began talking.

She was suddenly desperate to wipe that shocked look from his face. She didn't care if he'd come here just to ask her for a few repeat performances in the sack. She wanted that look on his face *to go away* because it made something inside her tighten with a pain she had never felt before.

'Tommy…yes, Tommy's my brother. I've been looking after him, really, for…all his life.' She paused, licked her dry lips and ran her fingers through her hair but she kept looking at him, trying to gauge what he was thinking. 'I never knew my dad,' she said jerkily. 'It was just me and Mum and then Tommy came along. Just the three of us but the responsibility…well, it fell on my shoulders from as far back as I can remember. My mum…our mother… she wasn't really into parenting. She was more into guys and having fun. When it came to taking responsibility for us…she just didn't have it in her. She was lovely and carefree and, as I got older, it felt as though she was…younger than me in a lot of ways.'

'You…have a mother…'

'I do, Nico. I have one of those.' Grace paused but he failed to fill the silence and so she ploughed on with the backstory she had withheld for such a long time. Nerves were skittering through her and she was perspiring.

'Enlighten me.' Nico's voice was barely audible.

'My mum had a couple of husbands. She was so

young when she had us and she was always in search for the right guy, always being knocked back. All I can remember is taking care of her, picking her up when she was down. She didn't like cooking, at least not the sort of stuff that kids should eat. We used to have pancakes for dinner and pizza for breakfast. Whatever came to hand. When I got old enough, I took over the business of making sure there was nutritious food on the table, at least most of the time.'

'And your brother?'

Grace could scarcely hear him and the expression on his face, while not as shocked, was blank, which almost felt worse.

'Tommy… Tommy suffered more from Cecily's lack of parenting skills.' Grace lost herself in the telling because it was cathartic and because she was desperate to tell him *everything*. 'I filled in the best I could but there was always disappointment when sports day arrived and Mum wasn't there. He was very talented on the playing field. Loved his rugby. He was climbing up the ladder, had been scouted and the future was looking bright but then he had an accident. A severe one and all those dreams came to an end.' Grace chewed her lip, remembering those painful days.

'I… I'm very sorry to hear that.'

'It was a very bad time all round. Worst of all was that just around then, as luck would have it, Mum found her guy. All that time, all those mistakes, but she found her guy. A great guy from Australia. A proper outback rancher who swept her off her feet. She married and then, very shortly after, emigrated to Australia.'

'She left you to take charge.'

'It happens.' Grace pressed her hands to her heated cheeks. 'Tommy was in hospital for ages and when he finally came out, he faced a long, hard struggle to get back on his feet, literally. Lots of physio, lots of setbacks and lots of therapy so that he could deal with what had happened.' She looked around her at the small, nondescript sitting room.

'I had to do my best for my brother. I got him somewhere small but specially adapted to suit his needs. And then the therapist. All private and none of that comes cheap, which is why I live here even though I've been paid a lot over the years. I'm babbling, I know, but, Nico…' Her voice trailed away into silence.

Nico listened. Every word was fresh hurt. He knew he shouldn't feel betrayed but he did, because she had a side to her, a *world* to her that she had denied him.

He thought of the flowers he had bought and the final hurdle he had overcome to let his defences down and thinking about that made him sick to the stomach.

He'd opened himself up, admitted his own vulnerability but he had fatally misread the signals. She had never allowed him in because what she felt for him had never been on a par with what he felt for her.

He had made a terrible mistake. Nico felt he was drowning under the weight of misplaced assumptions and a reckless optimism in something that had always been a chimera.

He stood up.

'It was a mistake coming here, Grace.' He moved towards the door and rested his hand on the doorknob and then said, over his shoulder, looking at her for the last time, 'When I leave here, you won't see me again. Don't try and contact me. The past has gone and that door is now closed for good.' He smiled heavily. 'Adieu for the last time.'

CHAPTER TEN

'SO WHAT ARE you going to do about it?'

Grace looked at her brother, the very same brother she had conditioned herself to believe would always be her responsibility. The very same brother, she now realised, who was perfectly capable of looking after himself. She smiled ruefully.

'He doesn't love me. Hey…since when are you the one dishing out the sensible advice?' But the smile had turned into a grin and for a split second she almost forgot her chaotically beating heart, the very heart that had been wrenched from her chest when Nico had walked out of the house.

Tommy looked at her seriously. 'This is a crossroads for us, sis. From now on, we're equals and, as such, I'm telling you that if you love this guy, then tell him, because if you don't you'll spend the rest of your life regretting it.'

'Okay.' Grace felt a slow fire begin to burn inside her. 'Maybe you're right. No. You *are* right. So, Tommy…' she walked as she talked, throwing words over her shoulder '…if you don't mind, I'm going to love you and leave you and…' She dashed to where he was sitting and hugged him tightly before standing back. 'Next time I see you, I want to see this girlfriend of yours. Understood?'

'Wouldn't have it any other way, sis.'

Of course, Grace knew where her boss lived. Like so many bits and pieces of information, it was just something else she had picked up along the way.

She didn't know whether he was going to return to his house or when.

She had no idea if, having walked out of her life, he might decide to return to the date he had abandoned.

She would wait.

She had enough on her mind to wait a thousand years and still have more thoughts to process.

The sprint to the Underground was breathing space she needed. She wanted to analyse everything he had said to her and every shifting expression on his face, but a sense of urgency jumbled all her thoughts.

He'd been so shocked to find out about Tommy and she could understand why. He had always been a man to value his privacy, but he had ended up sharing a great deal with her and so to discover that there had been major things she had chosen to keep to herself would have hurt.

She had babbled out all the confidences he had

been denied but she could remember the shutters that had slammed over his dark eyes, locking her out.

Grace knew that she had had the option to walk away. He had come bearing flowers and an invitation back to his bed, which was not what she wanted. If he had been hurt by the fact that she had guarded her private life from him, then *she* had had her fair share of suffering, knowing that she had fallen for someone who was incapable of returning her love.

The line could have been drawn underneath it all. Nico would never have returned. His adieu would truly have been final.

But Tommy had been right and she would have reached the same conclusion sooner rather than later. To live with regret was to live a half-life and she would have had a lot of regrets.

It was still and dark by the time she made it to Nico's palatial house in Kensington.

She had been there several times in the past. Twice to drop off urgently needed documents and another time for a Christmas gathering he had hosted for a handful of employees. It had been a grand occasion, with waiters everywhere and a classical quartet playing in the background. She could remember the way she had felt then…painfully aware of Nico in his black polo and black trousers and the woman who had followed him here, there and everywhere, looking at him with adoring puppy-dog eyes.

Why on earth she hadn't got the picture loud and

clear then and duly taken herself off to a dating site, Grace had no idea.

So long being careful and responsible had boxed her in. Her energies had gone into her job, and living a life outside that—outside Tommy and all the practicalities that went along with the care he had needed—had been sidelined. All those missed opportunities to meet a guy, have fun, see what the future might hold in store for her…not to mention to give Tommy the freedom from her stifling caretaking. He hadn't put it in so many words but she had understood without having to be told. Instead, she had remained in a holding bay, waiting for life to happen and daydreaming about Mr Impossible.

She had barely recognised her own crush on her boss for what it could dangerously mushroom into.

Now she was here, and she was going to deal with the fallout for all her poor choices whatever the outcome.

Of course, there was nothing convenient anywhere near his house, like a coffee shop. There were just other mansions with forbidding iron gates and precision-trimmed hedges tall enough to protect the occupants of the big houses from riff-raff's prying eyes.

In the absence of a key to his house, she did, fortunately, have the code to his side gate and she let herself in hoping no one saw her, because they would immediately call the police.

This was definitely not the sort of place where

random strangers were tolerated, least of all ones letting themselves in via side gates.

Of course, there was no one in. The darkness was a giveaway. Just the outside light illuminating the front door. She rang the bell anyway and, with the predictable lack of response, she went to the bench at the side and sat down. She was braced for the long haul. It was not yet nine in the evening. Thank goodness it wasn't too cold. A bit chilly but nothing her thick cardigan couldn't handle.

It was after eleven by the time Nico got back to his house. He'd left Grace and headed straight to the pub. It wasn't a gastropub with delusions of grandeur. It was one of the few proper pubs not a million miles from his house, because he wanted to walk back. A proper pub where a guy could go and drown his sorrows in a few honest-to-goodness bottles of strong beer.

He had to.

His mind was going crazy. He couldn't assimilate what had been thrown at him and even though he knew he was being an ass, because he, more than anyone else, should know that people were entitled to their privacy, he still felt bitterly hurt. Wounded to the very core. Wounded in places he hadn't even known existed.

The temperature had dropped. He felt the coolness penetrating his lightweight jacket as he clumsily pressed the buttons to the side gate. The walk had sobered him up, but he could still feel the effects of the beer he had drunk. Not enough to block out all his thoughts but enough for a definite improvement.

The sound to his left as he began heading up the Victorian paved path to his front door almost failed to penetrate.

The shape huddled on his bench registered a hell of a lot more and if the night air hadn't quite sobered him up, then the sight of someone on his property did the trick in record time.

And Nico's milk of human kindness was at an all-time low. He strode over at pace and reached for the collar of whoever was curled on his bench and then cursed with shock when the shape unfurled and he saw who it was.

She had gaped in surprise when he had shown up on her doorstep. Now it was his turn. He watched, stunned for a few seconds, as she rubbed her eyes and began sitting up.

'Jesus,' he muttered, swearing again. 'What are you doing on my bench, Grace? How long have you been here?'

'I'm cold,' she whispered by way of response.

Nico barely stopped to think. He swept her up in one fluid movement and carried her through the door and into the warmth of his sitting room, then he gently placed her on one of his wildly expensive leather sofas and stood back, arms folded, staring.

Grace looked up at him. Their eyes collided and she swallowed, at a disadvantage now that she was here, lying on his sofa while he towered over her with an expression that could freeze water.

She struggled to sit up, but her joints ached from how she had fallen asleep on the bench.

'Want to tell me why you're here?'

'I'm sorry.'

'You've come here to tell me that you're sorry? When I walked out your front door, Grace, I told you that I had no intention of ever seeing you again and I meant it.' His voice was cold and unforgiving. 'So what if I knew or didn't know about your brother, about the life you'd had? Not the end of the world. Trust me.'

'I know it's not the end of your world, Nico.'

'You're shivering.' He swore again, told her to stay put and returned seconds later with a glass. 'Drink this.'

Grace took the glass, drank the whisky and felt it burn through her nerves, giving her some much-needed strength.

'I wasn't keeping secrets from you,' she said quietly, nursing the glass.

'I told you—'

'Yes, that it doesn't matter. You came to my house to try and get me back into bed with you. I know that, Nico.' She watched his face darken into a scowl. 'You met Tommy and you were jealous but then you found out that he was my brother and you were hurt and I'm sorry about that.'

'You overestimate your position in my life, Grace.'

That felt like a body blow but she met his cool gaze without flinching. 'I've had a crush on you for years, Nico.' There, it was out in the open. It should have felt like a weight lifted from her shoulders because didn't they say that confession was good for the soul? Sadly, Grace just wanted the ground to open and swallow her up.

'I never thought it would ever come to anything because I always knew the sort of women you were attracted to. Racy blondes who enjoyed all the things money could buy. I wasn't a racy blonde so you were never going to be attracted to me. Ergo, having a crush on you was safe because nothing would ever come of it and I liked that because... I've spent all of my adult life being a coward.'

She looked at him as he shifted closer to sit on the sofa next to her.

This wasn't the equivalent of a welcome mat but at least it wasn't the sound of a door slamming in her face.

'I was brave when it came to looking after Mum and Tommy. I bore the brunt of all the hard work. Tommy was always the vulnerable one and I was always the strong one and, really, they both looked to me to do the caretaking. But I never had a chance to develop in all those areas where girls develop.'

'You weren't allowed *any* freedom to do what you wanted to do?'

The gentleness of his voice made tears prick the backs of her eyes for this was what she'd missed when he had withdrawn from her. She had thought she'd walked away from him, so it was ironic how much it had hurt when he had shown up unannounced only to retreat behind an impenetrable wall when he'd met Tommy and found out who he was.

'I had all the freedom in the world,' Grace said quietly. 'I just didn't know how to use it. My mother never chained me to the stove and forced me to cook and Tommy never asked me to help him with his homework or make him a packed lunch to take to school. I did it all because it just seemed to happen that way and then, somehow, I hit my teenage years and I found that I never learnt how to flirt or talk to boys or get invited to parties.' She smiled. 'Or even have confidence when it came to stuff like that. I had one boyfriend, which was a fumbling, clumsy affair, and it was so much easier to give up on the whole scary thing.'

'Go on,' Nico urged.

'Then, like I told you earlier, Mum married and moved to Australia not that long after Tommy's accident and my life seemed even more closed in. I started working for you and…yes, I developed a crazy crush on you.'

'I like that. I approve of crazy crushes.'

'I would have told you about Tommy and Mum… but there were lines between us, Nico. You were my boss. Even when we slept together, you were still my boss, and I was very conscious of that.' She paused and gazed at him with a thoughtful expression. 'No,' she admitted with painful honesty, 'it was more than that. Somewhere along the line, I realised that my crazy crush wasn't quite as harmless as I'd thought it would be. That's when I made up my mind to go on the Internet, find the life I'd been missing.'

'The nuisance lawyer... Victor? I remember his name.'

'That was my first foray.' She held his gaze sheepishly. 'I didn't expect to be caught out.'

'I'm glad I did. It showed me a side of you I think I always knew was there, waiting to get out. Tell me about this crush of yours and how it developed.'

'It got serious, Nico. I realised just how serious when I was on that wretched date, trying hard to make an effort and hating the fact that I was there, and, even worse, hating the fact that I wished it were you sitting opposite me. An impossible dream. A stupid impossible dream that had grown completely out of hand.' She sighed and yawned. The whisky had made her feel sleepy, but she was no longer cold and she could finally feel the weight being lifted from her shoulders.

'And then we went to that island.'

'Yes, we did.'

'We made love and it was everything making love is all about.'

'For me, it was falling in love, Nico. And that's why, even in those most intimate moments, when I wanted to rest my head on your shoulder and spill my soul, I didn't because I figured it would drive you away and I didn't want that to happen. I was a coward. I'd fallen in love with you and I wanted to do everything within my power to hang onto you for as long as I could. I was proud. I was greedy.'

'You fell in love with me…'

'That's what I came here to say. I couldn't bear the thought of you walking away and never knowing what was in my heart.'

'Oh, Grace…'

'I know what you're going to say. You're going to tell me that you can't return the feeling and I understand. I've always understood that what I felt for you would never come to anything.'

'In your search for a job,' Nico said gravely, 'I hope you haven't thought about going into fortune telling.'

'What do you mean?'

'I came to your house earlier because I wanted to tell you much the same thing.' He smiled wryly. 'Different backstory but there you go—we've ended up on the same page and maybe it was always going to be that way.'

Suddenly wide awake, Grace straightened and looked at Nico with urgency, although underneath the urgency there was still a thread of caution, guarding against believing something that sounded too good to be true.

'I don't understand,' she breathed.

'You do, Grace. I'm in love with you. I never thought it could happen to me. I've always told myself that I would never allow my emotions to wreak havoc with a cool head. My uncle—well, never mind that in the end I didn't know him, only knew of the reputation that lay in tatters after his exile—shaped my way of thinking. He represented everything that could go wrong when you lacked discipline. I looked at my own father and saw the opposite. An ordered life with ordered choices. He was the cool, calm and collected half of the coin where Sander was the other, and then I made my own youthful mistake.

'I fell for a girl who turned out to be just the sort of demanding woman I had spent a lifetime being warned against. In no uncertain terms I was warned that the woman who ended up at my side for the long haul would have to be someone who understood that I wasn't like anyone else. My father had his own empire and was responsible enough to put his employees first and I had my own and would have to do the same. There would be no time to pander to a woman who wanted all of me. I was too young to see that travelling down one road did not preclude the other. To be in charge didn't automatically mean making sure you never gave your emotions away. Falling in love didn't necessarily entail throwing yourself under the bus and giving in to a life of chaos. I look back on my parents and I can see now that while it may have been an arranged marriage of sorts, it was also a true love match.'

'You had such a varied, colourful love life, Nico...'

'Because I was happy to divide myself into two halves. The first would be the man who played the field and had fun and the second would be the man who gave that up and married a woman who didn't make demands, who left me to put work at the forefront of my life. Hot and cold, black and white, nothing in between. But, my darling, even while I was busy making those choices you were there, and little did I ever suspect that every minute of every day spent with you undermined all my grand plans for my future. Making love to you…it was different from anything I'd ever done before, fulfilling in ways I never dreamed imaginable and, of course, now I know why. I wasn't having sex, I was touching…tasting…*being* with a woman I had fallen hopelessly in love with.'

'So does that mean you forgive me for not telling you about Tommy?'

'On one condition…'

'What's that?'

'No more secrets between us. We talk about everything and anything all the time. Doubts, fears, hopes and dreams…we share everything.'

'I think I can agree to that…'

'And one other thing.'

'That's two conditions!' But she laughed, her eyes gently teasing him, filled with the love she had been so careful never to reveal.

'You marry me. As soon as possible. I want to start our lives together without waiting because I can't live without you.'

'I can definitely…' Grace flung herself at him, the man she'd loved for so long '…agree to that.'

EPILOGUE

GRACE LOOKED AT herself in the full-length mirror of the bedroom and smiled.

She twisted to one side, then to the other. Outside, winter was gathering in cold and darkness even though it was only a little after six in the evening.

Nico was due back any minute, and just thinking about that lock in the front door, and the decisive tread of his footsteps as he entered the lovely old cottage in Richmond they had chosen together a little over a year ago, made her heart thump.

The old, familiar feeling, a love that was so deep and so true that just thinking about him and knowing that she was the only person in the world to really see what lay inside him, made her shiver with pleasure.

Sometimes, she stopped and was amazed all over again at how much had happened in such a short space of time.

He hadn't been joking when he'd told her that he wanted their lives together to start right away.

'But a wedding takes ages to sort out,' Grace had

told him a little dubiously, but, as neither of them had wanted anything at all extravagant, it had been remarkably straightforward to arrange.

They had gone back to the island for it and had been welcomed warmly by the new owners of Sander's hotel and by the staff who remembered them from when they had last been there.

Old memories and new ones being shaped. Grace had looked around her to the turquoise sea gently lapping on sand as powdery as icing sugar, with the sun a setting orange ball sinking behind the indigo horizon. The assembled guests had been as struck as she had been by the beauty of the place as she and Nico had exchanged wedding vows.

Her floaty cream dress had reminded her of how she had felt that first time on the island, when she had dumped the starchy work clothes and slipped into the light, soft summer dresses she had bought, and she had blushed when her husband-to-be had looked at her with such love and tenderness that it had brought a lump to her throat. Had he read what she'd been thinking?

His parents had been there and that had been moving as they had touched base with the people Sander had grown to love.

They'd both kept in touch with him, as it turned out, and, much as they had pleaded for him to return to the fold, he had flatly refused, preferring the peace of the island.

Her mother had come as well, along with her step-father, and Tommy with his fiancée.

It had been a small affair. Relatives, friends… they had stayed at one of the five-star hotels in Nassau and she and Nico had remained back at Sander's hotel, as they privately called it.

'It's not where I started to love you,' Nico had whispered, on that first night after they had married on the beach, when everyone had been shuttled back to the main island, 'because that was something that started a long time before. But this place will always be special because it will always be where I touched you for the first time.'

When Grace thought back to the huskiness in his voice when he'd said that and the love in his eyes, she got a tingle of absolute contentment and a happiness that was as deep as an ocean inside her.

She heard the sound of the front door opening and she sprinted down the stairs just as Nico was shrugging off his coat.

'When are you going to stop doing this to me?' he murmured, moving towards her as she moved towards him.

'What's that?'

'Making me wish that my working day was shorter?' He grinned and pushed her hair back and then held her at arm's length and inspected her. 'I'm sensing something different about you this evening. New dress?'

Grace nodded. Now that she was working from home, editing a financial magazine, she had time to dash to the shops and, yes, the dress was new.

'I thought men weren't supposed to notice those things.' She grinned and spun round, pulling him towards the kitchen, where the table had been elaborately set, at which point he stopped in his tracks and turned her to look at him.

'First…' he grinned back at her and dropped kiss on the side of her mouth, and then, as though giving it a bit more thought, he kissed her thoroughly until she was all hot and bothered '…I'm unique, as I keep reminding you, and second, you need to tell me what's going on, because if you don't I'm going to start thinking that I might have forgotten something important.'

'I have a surprise for you.' Grace led him to the table where a slender box was wrapped with a ribbon round it and she watched as he held it aloft for a few puzzled seconds before peeling back the wrapping.

Then he smiled and the smile got wider and, when he looked at her, his dark eyes were ablaze.

'My day just got a whole lot better,' he growled, pulling her towards him and holding her close, so close that she could feel the beating of his heart under the crisp white shirt.

He held up the positive pregnancy stick and then looked at her and laughed with delight.

'A family. My darling, I can't wait. You've made

me the happiest man on earth and I will treasure you
till my dying breath.'

As I will you, Grace thought with overflowing
love. *As I will you...*

* * * * *

Couldn't get enough of
A Week with the Forbidden Greek?
*Then you'll be sure to fall in love with
these other stories by Cathy Williams!*

Claiming His Cinderella Secretary
Desert King's Surprise Love-Child
Consequences of Their Wedding Charade
Hired by the Forbidden Italian
A Baby Confession to Bind Them

Available now!

WE HOPE YOU ENJOYED
THIS BOOK FROM

⊕HARLEQUIN

PRESENTS

Escape to exotic locations where passion knows no bounds.

Welcome to the glamorous lives of royals and billionaires, where passion knows no bounds. Be swept into a world of luxury, wealth and exotic locations.

8 NEW BOOKS AVAILABLE EVERY MONTH!

#4057 CARRYING HER BOSS'S CHRISTMAS BABY
Billion-Dollar Christmas Confessions
by Natalie Anderson

Violet can't forget the night she shared with a gorgeous stranger. So the arrival of her new boss, Roman, almost has her dropping an armful of festive decorations. *He's* that man. Now she must drop the baby bombshell she discovered only minutes earlier!

#4058 PREGNANT PRINCESS IN MANHATTAN
by Clare Connelly

Escaping her protection detail leads Princess Charlotte to the New York penthouse of sinfully attractive Rocco. But their rebellious night leaves innocent Charlotte pregnant...and with a Christmas proposal she *can't* refuse.

#4059 THE MAID THE GREEK MARRIED
by Jackie Ashenden

Imprisoned on a compound for years, housemaid Rose has no recollection of anything before. So when she learns superrich Ares needs a wife, she proposes a deal: her freedom in exchange for marriage!

#4060 FORBIDDEN TO THE DESERT PRINCE
The Royal Desert Legacy
by Maisey Yates

If the sheikh wants Ariel, his promised bride, fiercely loyal Prince Cairo *will* deliver her. But the forbidden desire between them threatens *everything*. Her plans, his honor and the future of a nation!

#4061 THE CHRISTMAS HE CLAIMED THE SECRETARY

The Outrageous Accardi Brothers

by Caitlin Crews

To avoid an unwanted marriage of convenience, playboy Tiziano needs to manufacture a love affair with secretary Annie. Yet he's wholly unprepared for the wild heat between them—which he *must* attempt to restrain before it devours them both!

#4062 THE TWIN SECRET SHE MUST REVEAL

Scandals of the Le Roux Wedding

by Joss Wood

Thadie has not one but two reminders of those incredible hours in Angus's arms. But unable to contact her twins' elusive father, the society heiress decides she must move on. Until she's caught in a paparazzi frenzy and the security expert who rescues her is Angus himself!

#4063 WEDDING NIGHT WITH THE WRONG BILLIONAIRE

Four Weddings and a Baby

by Dani Collins

When her perfect-on-paper wedding ends in humiliation, Eden flees...with best man Remy! Their families' rivalry makes him *completely* off-limits. But when their attraction is red-hot, would claiming her wedding night with Remy be so very wrong?

#4064 A RING FOR THE SPANIARD'S REVENGE

by Abby Green

For self-made billionaire Vidal, nothing is out of reach. Except exacting revenge on Eva, whose family left a painful mark on his impoverished childhood. Until the now-penniless heiress begs for Vidal's help. He's prepared to agree...*if* she poses as his fiancée!

*Read on for a sneak preview of
Dani Collins's next story for Harlequin Presents,*
Wedding Night with the Wrong Billionaire

"It's just us here." The words slipped out of her, impetuous, desperate.

A distant part of her urged her to show some sense. She knew Micah would never forgive her for so much as getting in Remy's car, but they had had something in Paris. It had been interrupted, and the not knowing what could have been had left her with an ache of yearning that had stalled her in some way. If she couldn't have Remy, then it didn't matter who she married. They were all the same because they weren't him.

"No one would know."

"This would only be today. An hour. We couldn't tell anyone. Ever. If Hunter found out—"

"If Micah found out," she echoed with a catch in her voice. "I don't care about any of that, Remy. I really don't."

HPEXP1022

"After this, it goes back to the way it was, like we didn't even know one another. Is that really what you want?" His face twisted with conflict.

"No," she confessed with a chasm opening in her chest. "But I'll take it."

He closed his eyes, swearing as he fell back against the door with a defeated thump.

"Come here, then."

Don't miss
Wedding Night with the Wrong Billionaire.

Available December 2022 wherever
Harlequin Presents books and ebooks are sold.

Harlequin.com